Table of Contents

ADDITIONAL CREDITS

Editing by M.A. Hinkle (www.lesscourtauthorservices.com)

Cover and Promotional Art by Samantha Santana (www.amaidesigns.com[1])

Proof Reading by Kirk Waite (Rare Bird Beta Reading)

1. http://www.amaidesigns.com/

Thank you!

I want to especially thank M.A. Hinkle for her amazing skills and support in getting this story into amazing shape and really helping me make it shine.

And I want to thank Jennifer Conklin, because she is my frond to the ond and puts up with my Shatnering and is a wonderful, special, beautiful-soul-having supportive brain twin. I love you lots.

And Alec and Spawn... Thank you for putting up with me angsting over my imaginary friends. And for not leaving me alone in the dark on a rock in the middle of the ocean. I love you lots too but in a very different way.

Potential Trigger and Content Note:

This book contains potentially triggering subject matter including discussion of death, violence, genocide (mentioned, not described, of fantasy based society).

CHAPTER ONE

It's beginning to look a lot like fuck this.

ROWAN

Madam Lucinda Frost, matriarch of the Frost clan and a real Witch (seriously, I'm not being mean—she was a legit Witch, had a certificate and everything) swanned into the study, double-fisting tumblers of something amber and hopefully alcoholic. "You're not supposed to be here."

"Weird. That's not what the invitation said," I answered.

"Smartass; I like that in a man. Here. I saw you heading this way after the whole," she made a loose gesture with her own tumbler and shuddered, "*thing* downstairs and thought you might need one of these."

"Thanks." I took a small sip; it's never wise to *refuse* a Witch's hospitality, but it's also dangerous to *accept* a Witch's hospitality. The paradox of living in a magical community. You had to accept that, at some point, you were going to get a tiny bit poisoned. You just had to hope you could shake it off or had an antidote before the embarrassing side effects kicked in.

And, after spending the better part of an hour listening to one Witch after another rail on about how only *real* Witches should be allowed the use of magic, how only *real* Witches had any right to vote on the Revelation, I was pretty much down for whatever was in that cup, so long as it took the edge off my mood. "Oh, mead!"

She saluted me with her drink, then took a much bigger sip. "I had to hide it in scotch glasses. Otherwise, my daughter-in-law would've been in a tizzy over me getting into the wine for the ritual tonight." She smiled, staring into the depths of her drink. "I'm waiting for the day she can't control a situation to her exact liking and the top of her head flies clean off."

"I'm surprised my being here didn't cause her untimely demise."

Madam Frost tipped her glass gently in my direction, not bothering to hide her sharp grin before taking another sip.

The mead was delicious. Sweet, smooth, a little herbal. Like everything to do with the ritual was bound to be, it was enchanted and sent tendrils of warmth through every bone and vein in my body. I was drinking the perfect summer moment.

The thought made me snort softly. Madam Frost watched me with a keen, knowing smile. "Let me guess," I smirked at her. "You were in charge of the guest list?"

She lifted one elegant shoulder in a shrug. "It's my home. And I'm the one on the Grand Council, not her."

The faint note of childlike petulance in her voice charmed me. Lucinda Frost was a terrifying figure in the supernatural community: notoriously intimidating, imperious, and, worst of all, *always* right. Like, always. Not in the, 'Oh, they're always right' way people say when someone is an asshole, and it's easier to let them have their way and pretend they're correct to save yourself the grief.

No, Lucinda Frost was always, always right. Her magic was subtle, ancient, and powerful. Popular rumor said even werewolves feared her. Which was absolute bullshit because werewolves weren't real.

No, really. Totally not real.

Trust me, I'm a Demon. I know things.

"So, if you're on the council—"

"If?"

"Excuse me. *Since* you are on the council, you know why she's twitchy about my presence." I took another drink of the mead. It was amazing. Witch magic was at work with each mouthful I took, but I didn't much care. Was that part of it, making me lose my inhibitions enough to get myself in trouble? Though what would I do to cause a scene? That was the question. "The question of the big reveal to humans is up for a vote at the Winter Solstice, and Demons are the wrench in the works, aren't we?"

She inhaled slowly, rolling her now-empty glass back and forth between her palms. We were in the upstairs study, far enough away from the crowd gathered in the downstairs areas to muffle their voices down to a dull hum, but close enough the tingle and zaps of a hundred kinds of magic made my skin crawl. Each person I'd met since arriving at the Summer Solstice festivities and council meeting had been less than pleased to see me.

I admit I wasn't impressive—tall, lanky, hair with a mind of its own, glasses I could never keep clean...I looked like a college student on a three-day study bender and not a successful business owner, much less a Demon from a long line of Demons, down from Ashmodai himself. Maybe they'd have been more welcoming if I'd swanned in like my brother, Ellery, all sharp suits and brooding good looks, a hint of danger in every move, magic subtle and used sparingly. People never guessed he was still terrified of spiders and had his childhood quilt tucked up under his silk-covered pillow in his massive Alaska king-sized bed.

"I will acknowledge," Madam Frost said when the silence had stretched too thin, like taffy about to snap between us, "your presence was unexpected for the rest of the lot downstairs. But it is necessary. If we are to make ourselves known to the mundanes again, we must *all* make ourselves known."

"Are you more concerned with fairness, or are you afraid Demons might be able to stay under the radar if we're not part of the Revelation?" Another sip of summer down the gullet, and I was loose-limbed, smiling. Not drunk, simply full of sweet warmth and the swell of happiness from sinking your toes into soft grass, bending and cool beneath your feet.

She lifted her glass again, full once more through a bit of her own unseen deviltry. "I am a complex woman, Mr. Hebert. Your grandmother Heliotrope could have told you as much."

"She did. Many times." Using far more colorful language.

"Heliotrope was quite singular," Madam Frost's birdlike gaze pinned me again. "She was quiet if one did not know her. I knew her, however. And she was not shy in her belief that Demons have a place on the council as full members."

"I—"

"Lola?" The door to the study swung open on soundless hinges, revealing the tall, sturdy form of Whitaker Frost, Madam's only grandchild and a man so pretty I might have died if I looked at him too long. He glanced at me, and my face flushed hot and red, a shade I'd come to call Shame Tomato over years of being a generally awkward person. For a small moment, I thought maybe he'd smile at me, wink, perhaps. *Some* sign he remembered our encounter at the Equinox only a few months before, when hours of eye-fucking culminated in one of the hottest half-hours of my life.

He barely glanced at me. Though I took some small measure of hope that the pink tinge on his cheeks was for me and not because he'd been dipping into the sacramental wine, too.

"Lola?" I asked, barely managing to keep my gaze focused on Madam Frost. She smirked all too knowingly at me, giving me a short *hurry up* nod in the direction of my half-full drink.

"When he was small, Whitaker heard adults call me Lucinda and couldn't say it himself. Hell of a lisp." Her tone was mock-confidential.

"Lola," Whitaker ground out through a stiff, forced smile, "Mother is making noises about finalizing placements for the ritual. She's asked me to come find you and is threatening to look for you herself if I return empty-handed."

I toasted her with my nearly empty glass. "Don't keep your fans waiting, Lola," I teased.

She huffed something quite uncomplimentary under her breath but tempered it with a wink.

"Will you be attending the ritual part of the afternoon, or will I not see you until the council meeting after?" she asked as she reached Whitaker's side.

Bracing myself, I turned to look at her in the doorway. I knew there was no way to avoid glancing directly at Whitaker Frost, so I figured to avoid any unpleasant expression of lust. Like that weird little strangled noise I absolutely did not make when I saw how intently he was staring at me with those hooded, dark eyes of his. The same look he'd given me before we gave in to our mutual lust back at the Equinox.

"Ah." I cleared my throat, but Madam Frost's cackle told me she knew damn well what was going on with me. "The ritual isn't my cup of tea," I finally said. "I'll take a spin around the grounds until it's over."

She nodded curtly, all business once again. "It was a pleasure talking with you, Mr. Hebert." Distantly, the silvery sound of bells wove through the murmur and hum of voices. "Oh, Hell, your mother never could hold her horses," she snapped at Whitaker. "Come on, then!" She was off at a near gallop down the corridor, heading for the stairs and leaving Whitaker to linger in the doorway.

"I'm surprised to see you here." He took a few steps backward in the direction his grandmother had fled. "I didn't think you'd show."

"Well. I was invited." I had the embarrassing urge to produce my invitation, folded and worn from so many examinations in the month leading up to the gathering as I tried to convince myself it was legit and not some weird joke by my cousins. *Were you hoping I wouldn't or wishing I would?*

He nodded. "That's...good." The bells sounded again, louder this time, and he frowned. "Well. Yes."

I raised a hand in farewell, but he was already gone. "Ugh, what the Hell?" I muttered, flopping down onto one of the wingback chairs. My glass was empty. The summer I'd drunk had already dissipated, leaving me with the crunchy, damp sensation of early autumn leaves falling before it was really dry enough to be pretty and still wet enough to be gross and slimy.

I waited until the hum and zing of magic downstairs shifted away, my skeleton no longer feeling like it wanted to climb out of my skin to get away from the electric threat. Then I made my way down to the front garden, a neat little knotwork number featured in *Old Money Weekly* or something similar. My mother had a subscription for the articles, but I knew she was really into the garden porn.

The ritual was to be held in the pavilion (in case the house, Downton Abbey's lovechild with Hogwarts, didn't tip you off, the Frosts' freaking pavilion should tell you they had ridiculous amounts of money). The area was several minutes' walk down the back of the property towards a large, natural pond. The property itself was a higgledy-piggledy patchwork of meadows, old groves, surprisingly barren areas where nothing but rocks seemed to proliferate, softly wet swaths near the water, and, somewhat disconcertingly, a very misty area, only visible from the corner of my eye. It disappeared entirely when I tried to get a better look.

A few other guests lingered in the garden, perched on benches or under arbors hung heavily with drying herbs and creeping vines. Bees buzzed low and lazy, dipping into the fat flowers bursting from the hedgerows around us. Most of the others skipping the ritual portion of the gathering were Druids, who had their own way of celebrating the Solstices, and a handful of Sidhe or Sidhe-born, who had to be Unseelie judging by the wide but respectful berth they were given by the other guests.

I was the lone Demon in attendance. Even the sour-faced Sidhe with the jaggedly pointed ears and aura of *fuck off with your sunshine and light bullshit* didn't want to speak with me, the most non grata of personas. I gave a staring Faerie a nod and tight smile, slipping past them and out of the knot garden and into an elaborate hedge maze. It was a basic spiral, but the hedges themselves had been trained into ornate twists and complicated shapes, charms for furring perspective woven into their knotted branches. It was, I guessed, supposed to make entering into a contemplative, meditative state easier as you followed the spiral inward, but it instead made me feel slightly drunk and not a little annoyed.

"It's better if you don't fight it."

I stopped. *Great. The bushes talk.*

"Sorry, didn't mean to scare you. I'm just... Hold on a sec." The bushes to my right rustled, shivered, and then an arm shot through, followed by a shoulder and finally a head in a bizarre birth tableau. Whitaker smiled sheepishly before fighting his way out of the tangled shrubs and stepping onto the path in front of me. "Sorry, I didn't mean to scare you," he repeated. "I saw you heading in here and wanted to have a quick word before you got to the middle. I took a wrong turn back at the lavender arch myself," he added.

"I'd think you'd be familiar with the path," I said, feeling my face turn a shade called Awkward Strawberry.

He shrugged. "I don't come out here often. It changes so much anyway. When I was younger, I tried to memorize the patterns, but by the time I got it down, the damn thing would shift again." Pausing, he gave me an assessing look. "I'm sorry, I know it all sounds crazy but—"

"I'm familiar with magic." My voice held only the tiniest hint of bitterness. "Despite what most Witches seem to think, Demonborn *do* have some idea how Witch-magic works. Your grandmother is known all over for her green thumb. If you told me she had a greenhouse full of plants performing the entirety of *A Chorus Line*, I wouldn't be surprised."

Whitaker snorted softly, looking down at his hands, where broken leaves had left green streaks, and small sticks had scratched up beads of blood. "Well, this magic isn't hers." He nodded at the maze around us. "It's older than her, if you can believe that." Very faintly, the silvery bells sounded again, and he sighed. "Look, I wanted to apologize for being rude earlier. I wasn't expecting you to be upstairs with her. And after what happened downstairs with the others...well, I wanted to let you know that not all Witches hate Demonborn."

"So long as we mind our manners and don't try to get ahead of ourselves?" The snark bubbled up with no warning. Well, maybe a tiny bit of warning. Since the whole meet and greet debacle, I'd been on edge, just waiting for a chance to vent my spleen. Lucky Whitaker was in my spleen's path, it seemed, despite a large part of my brain telling me to throw myself at him and start ripping clothing off.

"I didn't say—"

"No," I sighed, "you didn't. You didn't have to. You were downstairs while your guests were cornering me, though." I finally looked him in the eye, not just at a spot past his left ear. He was so freaking beautiful, and something inside me wanted to wrap around him, breathe him in. I hated how strong the pull was. It made me feel weak. Small. Less. *Steady on, Rowan.* "You didn't do a thing."

He drew back. "I know. I just—"

"I know. You just."

The bells rang again, louder. Madam Frost's voice drifted on the breeze, no doubt magically amplified. "Guests attending the small council session, please meet in the Ivory Ballroom."

I smiled thinly at Whitaker. "I hope that's merely the color scheme and not the building material."

He let me get several feet away, heading back the way I came, before he called out to stop me. "Rowan! Wait!"

"I don't want to be late for the meeting."

"Let me help you out of here, at least. I wanted to talk to you about the meeting before it started. You should know what's going to happen."

"I have a fairly good idea." I quickened my pace. My heart was pounding, and it had nothing to do with speed walking through the maze.

"I don't think you're being fair to me." He was much closer than I'd expected. If I went any faster, I'd be running. "I want you to know before we get in there—"

"*I'm* not being fair to *you*? I spent the better part of an hour being derided and harassed by your guests, by members of the Grand Council." My voice shook, more anger and shame than exertion. Whitaker made a sound, something like a sigh or a grunt.

"I thought earlier..." he began but trailed off as we twisted and turned through the maze. "Was I mistaken, then? There wasn't a spark between us?"

"A spark?" I stopped but didn't turn to face him. I could feel him close behind me, the faintest breath of cool air always lingering around him, teasing the back of my neck. "Now it's you who's not being fair," I muttered. "You know damn well that I...that what happened between us wasn't out of boredom or a...a fuck-you to the Witches or something."

"I'd wondered," he admitted softly. "I'd hoped it wasn't. But sometimes, being around this council crap really plays mind games with me." He laid his fingers on my shoulder, barely touching. "Rowan..."

I felt awkward and off-balance. I was there to do my duty to the Demonborn, not schmooze with Witches, I reminded myself sternly. Even if the Witch was really painful levels of adorkably hot. Like...ugh. Hot. Whitaker Frost was not only a walking wet dream (okay, ew, sorry) but the firstborn son of the Frost clan. The most powerful Witch clan in the United States and pretty much *the* Grand Council. Sure, they let other people join, but we had to play by their rules. And their biggest rule? Demonborn should not be seen or heard. And if they absolutely *had* to put up with us, they'd do it under sufferance and make sure we all knew it was an imposition.

Thankfully, whatever magic the maze had didn't decide to be capricious, and it let me follow the path I'd taken in without shifting me around. I joined the throng of people heading into the house, Whitaker at my heel. He peeled off once we entered the massive ballroom where Witch-lights glowed in the air overhead, and the walls shone with a soft white-gold glow, nothing like ivory. Whitaker headed for the top of the room, leaving me to figure out where I was supposed to sit on my own.

One long table had been set up down the middle of the room, dark wood polished to a glossy sheen. I was afraid to touch it and leave my sweaty fingerprints on the pristine surface. Small cards denoted who sat where, but thankfully Madam Frost had directed some of her household staff to show guests to seats and save some time; otherwise, we'd have been wandering around the table for miles until we each found our marked spot.

I was, unsurprisingly, one of the farthest from the head of the table. Whitaker was near the front, not one of the leaders of this meeting but obviously an honored guest, seeing as how we were in his family home. I couldn't make out his expression from down the table, but I could feel his eyes on me while everyone settled in. Beside me, a tiny twist of a Witch with hair the precise color of overcooked oatmeal and a smell to match settled in atop several plump cushions provided for their comfort. They grunted at me, gave me an intense onceover, and promptly turned to the Sidhe on their other side. Sighing, I looked over at the Witch on my right, who was doing a stellar job of pretending I didn't exist. In fact, they seemed to be in some sort of silent communication with the Witch across from me, the two of them staring intently at one another and unmoving.

Fantastic.

I fiddled with my name card. I was apparently now Roland Herbert instead of Rowan Hebert. The glass of water at my place was the only one not charmed to remain cold, I noticed, the condensation already leaving a gross ring on the beautiful table. A quiet staff member moved down the room, placing small plates of delicate pastry in front of each guest. Mine was the only one broken and crunched into crumbly pieces. Another staff member deposited expensive pens and notepads for each of us. My pen was leaky, and the notepad was missing half the pages, torn out roughly and leaving jagged bits of paper protruding.

To top it all off, someone nearby whispered, "Demon slime," just as a zip of something painful scored a line on the back of my hand. A flutter of movement raced along my end of the table, people shifting and waiting, watching. They wanted to see what I would do when provoked because, even among the magical sorts, stereotypes held a lot of sway.

Great, I was back in junior high. I wouldn't be surprised if I walked out of the meeting with my voice breaking and a huge spot on my chin, to complete the transition back to my early teens to go along with the bullying.

Opening up just a tiny bit, letting them feel a twist of pain in their muscles, a racing fear straight through their nerves, would have been easy, even felt good. Demon magic was old, older than Witches, primal in ways Witch magic can't imagine. Making this entire table of council members fear little ol' me would take minimal effort. They would shut up about Demonborn being 'lesser,' something foul and twisted. They would know how we could make them bend.

And it would fuck me over big time.

Ugh.

I swallowed down hard on the rising bubble of anger, of shame-filled rage forcing its way past my better judgment and focused on my fingers pressed flat on the table, steaming.

At the far end of the table, Madam Frost rose, holding a gleaming silver bell, and rang it once. A soft rush of cold air raced down the table, heavy with the smell of snow and woodsmoke and something dark green and herbal. It cut the warm aroma of summer lingering over us all, paring it away and leaving a near-metallic sharpness in its wake. The golden glow of the walls brightened to blue-white, sun on snow, and, as the chime of the bell faded, the room settled into a quiet, watchful mood.

"Though there are many months before the next Solstice, we must begin our planning now. The Winter Solstice will be a turning point for our community as a whole, and our clans and tribes individually." For a lingering, surprising moment, her gaze met mine. Her expression was indiscernible from my position at the table, but something moved through me, a seeking tendril I thought might be her bringing a settling a calmness in its wake. "If we are to move forward in this discussion," she continued, her ringing tones silencing anyone who might protest, "it is imperative we include *all* members of our community."

Her implication was clear.

Every face turned towards me.

Shit.

"First speaker, Whitaker Frost. My grandson and current liaison-in-waiting for whenever we make contact with the human faction."

Whitaker stood as Madam Frost sat. Not looking up, he fidgeted with a stack of cards in his hands. He lacked the confident air I'd seen in various gatherings and even in passing, the few times he'd stopped by my store while he was in town. He shifted between his feet, cleared his throat, and finally straightened, slipping into the posture I was more familiar with. The one creeping into my fantasies some nights, where he'd appear in my office and demand to know...well, something, and just be all businesslike and smooth and—a

Fuck, everyone was staring at me again.

"Um," I murmured, "I'm sorry, what was that?"

Whitaker addressed me directly. "I said, while I respect my grandmother's wishes for the future of this council and the Revelation, I fear she is being shortsighted. The Demonborn have been so long removed from meaningful participation in council meetings and interactions with the larger magical community that the general sentiment amongst the community is one of distrust. As things stand..." He paused. Could he feel the hot shame and anger washing through me? "As things stand, we must either delay the Revelation until things improve between Demonborn and the rest of the community, or we must move forward without the Demonborn."

The sheer amount of effort it took not to bolt from the room when the fighting began left me feeling tight and awkward. My entire body was one giant spasm of *run run run* while my brain belayed that order, forcing me to sit still and let the vitriol bubble around me, hateful words slicing into my middling self-control. I—well, Demons—had a few allies in the council. Primarily Madam Frost, much to the shock of the others in the room, and a few of the Sidhe, who remembered more than the others had forgotten about Demonborn and our history, how we had taught magic to a few worthy humans back when things were still fairly new.

Being reminded of this did not endear Demons to the others.

"Seriously," I finally barked at them all over the shouting and snarling. My eroding control finally collapsed under the weight of the fighting. "Decide if you hate us because we taught humans how to protect themselves or if you hate us because, without us, you wouldn't exist. Witches, that is. You lot," I waved at a few of the Sidhe and the one representative from the cryptid community, an odd man who wore a long, hooded coat even indoors that I suspected hid a pair of wings, "you'd have existed without Demons anyway. They," I turned back to the glaring Witches, "they would never have learned about magic without Demons. Deny it all you want," I added before anyone could start shouting again, "but you're lying to yourselves if you say otherwise."

I managed to walk calmly but quickly from the room before it exploded into noise again. I made it down to the front drive. Then I had to collapse and sit on the ground. The tang of winter from the council meeting still clung to me, and I closed my eyes, breathing it in deeply. I loved the Winter Solstice, but now I wondered if it'd be tainted for me forever, associating the smell of cold air and mistletoe and burning wood with the hate-fest of the small council meeting.

My stomach churned unpleasantly, the building headache behind my eyes threatening to crest into a tidal wave of a migraine. What the Hell had he been playing at? Trying to make nice before the meeting, then turning around and...*ugh*. My heart hurt, squeezed dry and flat. Had our encounter at the Equinox been some sort of joke, then? Had it been part of this plan? Get me feeling warm towards him, towards Witches in general, and maybe I wouldn't put up so much resistance?

I pressed my face into my palms, digging my nails into my skin just enough for the bite of pain to drag me away from the threatening tears.

"The meeting isn't over yet," Madam Frost said from somewhere above me. I tipped my head back. She stood on her porch steps, tall and imperious as Hera herself. "If you expect us to take the Demonborn seriously, get back inside and suck it up, Rowan Hebert."

"With all due respect, Madam Frost," I began, pushing myself painfully to my feet, "I don't think—"

"I'm well aware. Now. Inside." In a sweep of deep green and burnished gold, she turned and disappeared back into the house, leaving the faintest chill in her wake.

I slowly, grudgingly, followed her, settling into my seat once more as Egon, the head of the Witch council, droned on about bureaucratic bullshit. I tried to see if the faces around me were equally as bored as I was or if they were actually into it, but Whitaker's sweeping gaze arrested my own. He was staring at me, something I wished to think of as hunger on his face. Ugh.

I still wanted him and wanted him to want me. Then Egon said something, and Whitaker had to glance away to answer the question, leaving me feeling red and warm and uncomfortable. Quietly getting up from my chair again, I headed for the bathroom off the foyer to take care of business and splash cold water on my face.

"HEY."

Whitaker stood in the bathroom doorway.

"Um, hi," I replied.

"I wanted to explain myself. Explain why..."

I took a shallow breath. Swallowing down my anger as best I could, I met his gaze in the mirror. "Do it then. Make it good."

"I want you—Demonborns, I mean—in the Grand Council. You need to be able to vote on the Revelation. But as things stand..." Trailing off, he blew out a shaky breath. "As things stand, the rift between Demonborn and the rest of us is too great."

"What about the Equinox?" I asked, the question spilling out. "You didn't think the rift was too great while we were making out like horny teenagers behind the dining pavilion."

He shook his head, opened his mouth once or twice like he wanted words to happen. And then he was against me, pressing me back into the wall, our mouths crashing together. Frustration and lust warred for dominance, coming up tied in knots.

This, I decided, was the best part of the damned meeting.

CHAPTER TWO

Someone's chestnuts are about to be roasted.

WHITAKER

"Whitaker! Really!"

"Yes, really, Whitaker," I teased, unwinding my silk-blend scarf (fashionable in the city, absolutely useless in the valley) and looping it over one of the hooks nearest the door. "Seriously, Mother, I'm your firstborn, the one you wanted." Distantly, I felt the thrum of my sister Lydia's protest. "You'd think that fact alone would be enough for you to know it's really me." I leaned in to brush a kiss on my mother's powdered cheek, only to have her turn away pointedly, her lips pursed and eyes narrowed. Nobody gave a cold shoulder like my mother. "Oh, Gods, what now?" I sighed. "What did I do?"

"Do you have it?" she whispered loudly. "You're late, so you better have it with you!"

I patted my coat, where the package causing me to be over an hour behind schedule was tucked safely away from the cold and snow. "You know you live close enough to the city. One of you lot could've come down this week and picked it up yourselves. I wouldn't have had to take off early from work."

"You were coming here anyway," my mother dismissed airily, her mood already improving. "Come on, then. The meeting started an hour ago, and I've been stalling them." She swept away in a cloud of Caron Poivre and soft powder, her long skirts whipping in a breeze she never seemed to realize she conjured.

I hesitated before following her down the narrow corridor opening into the great room. I could hear the murmur of voices, sense the vibrations of many magics overlapping and sliding around one another. They all felt old, ancient in most cases. It never failed to remind me of hiding away under the stairs with Lydia when we were young and fancied ourselves as spies, trying to eavesdrop through the layers of spells and charms keeping conversations secret. Those thrums of magic hadn't changed in the handful of years since I was small enough to crawl under the staircase, and I doubted they'd change long after I'd turned to dust.

Before she reached the entrance, Mother turned and gave me an arched brow look to make Maggie Smith weep.

"I was going to stop by the kitchen." I patted the lump in my coat. You couldn't really ruin fruitcake, but keeping it tucked against my sweaty chest for much longer would definitely do nothing beneficial for it.

"Whitaker." Her teeth were clenched, cheeks wrenched into a smile that had to be painful. "Our guests are waiting."

Our guests? "Oh?"

She nodded, gesturing broadly with one hand, the other pressed to her stomach as if to quell particularly violent butterflies. "The council has been waiting for you to arrive, darling."

This was definitely double-plus ungood.

Slowly, I forced myself to move and trail after Mother into the stone-and-wood great room, part of the original home following the family around for generations. A dozen sets of eyes turned towards me, taking a moment to evaluate me, then dismiss me as nonthreatening. I raised one hand in a little wave, earning a heavy sniff from Egon, the head of our little Witch's council, before everyone turned their attention back to him. Egon droned on about the upcoming vote and logistics to ensure every clan, tribe, pack, and loosely associated band was present, and no one could claim to be left out.

Mother resumed her seat, carefully positioned near the hearth as befitting the lady of the house but not in a position of leadership before the council. Still, she put herself near Egon in her gilt-accented wingback chair with the velvet upholstery and subtle pearl insets. It was a power move, really, and I had to admire her for it.

I tried to catch her gaze with a *what the fuck, Mom* look. I found myself buffeted towards the outskirts of the room by a knot of diminutive Witches from a very distant branch of the tree, jostling for position on one of the low sofas circled up near the hearth.

I edged my way around the room towards my father, who looked half asleep, propped on one of the deep window seats overlooking the front drive. Snow fell thick and soft, a picture-perfect postcard image I knew had been arranged specifically for this council meeting, as there'd been no snow forecast for the rest of the week. "You bring it?" my father muttered, leaning towards me to whisper.

"Not you too," I groaned, letting my head thump gently against the window behind me. A few of the Wyrd sisters glared over the back of the sofa but snapped their attention back to Egon when he cleared his throat pointedly, sending a sharp look in my direction.

Father smirked. "It was all I could do to keep her from going down to the end of the road and meeting you as you came into town. She was sure you'd forget. You know how important this meeting is for her." He paused, then amended, "Well, to all of us, but you know how she likes her events."

I shifted the tightly wrapped package out from beneath my coat. "She didn't even give me a chance to get my kit off," I laughed softly, trying not to let the plastic and paper wrapping crinkle. Egon's throat clearing was more pointed this time.

"Sorry," I mouthed. "Sorry."

"I'm glad you finally made it," the oldest Witch in the western world said, his tone making it clear he felt anything but happy to see me. Egon had hated me ever since I hexed his youngest son to burst into song whenever he bragged, and Lord did that child brag a lot. It wouldn't have been much of a problem, except I forgot the counter hex, and Egon had had to come back from Lisbon on a red-eye to unravel my overly complicated hexwork. "I'm curious, and your parents had no answer for me...are you still friends with the Hebert clan?"

Dozens of sets of eyes were back on me again, sharp as talons. "I...no. Not in about six or seven years."

Eight. It had been eight years. And Egon knew it, the bastard.

His keen gray eyes narrowing, he stared me down. He wouldn't be so uncouth as to use a compelling charm on me in my parents' home, but the temptation was writ large on his face. I could practically see him racing through every law and bylaw, apothegm, rule, decree, dictum, ruling, statute, guideline, and suggestion in our very detailed and lengthy history. Finally, he settled back in the velvet Chesterfield armchair (my mother had a decorating theme, and she stuck with it) and smiled.

"As we are all aware, the Solstice is just ten days away. And we," he made a vague gesture, indicating the representatives of all of the major Witch families perched like eager puppies around him, "have been honored by the High Council with hosting the annual meeting. And I needn't remind everyone how dire the situation is." His gaze flickered over the assembled Witches, landing on me for barely a beat too long for me to be comfortable. His smile oozed back into place, and he gestured to my mother, not even deigning to turn his head. "Nanette, if you would?"

In a graceful waft of skirts and smiles, Mother rose, her magic smooth as silk, flowing over her guests in an age-old gesture of welcome. "As many of you are aware, the Frosts have long been keepers of the Solstice."

One of the Wyrd sisters muttered something about my mother under her breath, not entirely inaccurate. However, I did feel moved to defend her; she was still my mom, after all. I flicked the sister's ear. "Hey, do you mind?"

She raked a dark blue gaze over me from head to toe and back again, lingering in the middle. "Not at all. When this meeting's over, I can show you how little I mind."

I managed to withhold the shudder, but I think she caught on. Maybe it was the face I made. My father tugged on the back of my shirt, making me sit up once more. "Hush. Once your mother's done with her spiel, we can eat. I'm starving."

Mother expounding upon the Frost family’s fine heritage as Witches since the beginning of record history. More than a thousand years ago, we had been gifted the responsibility over the Winter Solstice by the Faerie Queen herself.

She was really good at selling the Frosts as some kind of amazing, considering she'd only been one for a bit over thirty years.

A small and bent Witch who looked exactly as if a knot of wood had come to life, decided hats were awesome, and donned a rather fetching green one to come and sit on the hassock in my family's great room spoke up. "That’s nice, Nanette, but let's get to the point, hm? You're hosting an open ritual this year, and you'd be honored for us to attend, blah blah blah, and then hold the council meeting and vote on the big reveal." The Witch rolled their eyes, dark, glittering sparks in their gnarled face. "Can we make this trot? I smell fruitcake, and I haven't eaten since the airport."

Mother was thoroughly disconcerted. She shot a mildly panicked look at Egon, who merely raised one elegant shoulder and flicked his fingers in a 'go on then' gesture. Mother smoothed her palms over her Hermes scarf and vintage blue gown before ratcheting her glossy smile up another few notches. "Yes, well, now that the cat is out of the bag," she said cheerfully, though the faintest smell of something burning scudded through the room, "I am thrilled to confirm it is, indeed, true! Egon has suggested we open our ancient ritual to you," she made a sweeping gesture I just knew she'd practiced, "the heads of all the Witch clans, modern and ancient. During the ritual, we will welcome the High Council leaders so we may hold the vote on the Grand Reveal." Another gesture, dancer-graceful and out of place in the meeting. "After the vote has been had, we will welcome the Solstice with the traditional bell ceremony, thus cementing the council's decision as well as reaffirming our ties to the ancient Wellspring of our gifts." She smiled sweetly. "All of us, not just the Frosts."

Beside me, Father tensed. Allowing the heads of the other clans to draw from the Wellspring was rare. It meant tying the clans together far more closely than they'd been in centuries. He shot me a quelling look and shook his head slightly. Later. Damn right, we'd discuss this later.

"Whitaker, darling, bring the box up here, would you?" Mother trilled. "I'd like to show the others our little surprise." She made a 'come here' motion, lowering her voice confidentially, playing to a bored audience. "When my dear mother-in-law died just after the autumnal Equinox, it fell to me...ah, my husband as her only child, that is, to hold the sacred instruments of our duty."

A weird little giggling feeling raced through me. "Um, Mother? A moment?"

"No," she said through her teeth, lips parted in a glossy red smile. Beside me, my father sighed a soft sound of resignation and gave me a nudge forward. The paper-and-foil-wrapped box in my hands was far heavier than it had any right to be, making my steps slow as I was summoned imperiously onward.

"It is not often the Solstice ritual has been opened," she said, ignoring a few not-so-muttered remarks from clan heads in attendance, "but it is our duty—all of us—in this time of potential upheaval to maintain our strong clan ties and present a unified front, reclaiming the ancient bonds the human world has unknowingly worked so hard to sever."

In truth, my great-great-grandfather started the tradition of the Frosts holding the ritual alone, without allowing the other clans to be present. Instead, he utilized proxies in the form of Faerie-cast bells, each one holding the name of a Witch clan. All were imbued with a single drop of blood from the clan leaders, except for a single small bell the size of my thumbnail. It was the Stranger's Silver, meant to hold a place for any newcomer who might join our ranks, any stranger who needed the protection of the Witch clans.

Witches are really freaking dramatic, in case you hadn't caught on.

Holding the package tightly to my chest, I reached my mother's side. Her smile was stiff and fixed, damn near predatory as she swung to face me. "Whitaker, don't tease our guests now. Let's have the box from your grandmother." She trilled one of her company laughs, reaching for the box and stopping just short of doing something drastic when I wouldn't let go. She pulled, setting her heels into the plush carpet. "When Lucinda passed on, the bells were sent to Whitaker for safekeeping."

"No, they weren't," I hissed, tugging back on the box.

"Not. Funny." She jerked once more, and the box popped out of my hands. A shiver of her magic raced over my fingers, a Hold Still, Child spell. Even if I wanted to, I wouldn't be able to snatch the box back for at least a few more minutes. Hands hanging useless at my sides, feet rooted, I could only watch in a mixture of second and firsthand embarrassment as my mother gently unwrapped the small box. "These have been in the Frost family for centuries," she murmured, folding back the thick white paper I'd wrapped over the box to protect it from the elements.

"They've been in Witch hands for centuries," the tiny, knotted Witch snapped. "The Frosts have held them for decades, but they belong to all of the clans, Nanette."

Egon waved a negligent hand at her. "We are prepared to let bygones be bygones here, aren't we? In the face of the upcoming changes to our community—all of our communities," he added with a hint of a grudge. We Witches liked to think we were the only supernatural beings out there, but a laundry list of creatures would beg to differ.

Mother hesitated as she discovered the plain white box beneath the wrapping. "This is a different box."

"Um, well, they have to use a fresh one with each order. Health codes and all that."

Mother raised her eyes to meet mine. The room was so quiet I could hear Mother's molars grinding. "Whitaker."

"To be fair," I said with all the charm I could muster, "it's really good fruitcake."

"WALK ME THROUGH THIS," Egon said tiredly, "one more time." The meeting had come to a screeching (in the case of Mother, literally screeching) halt. On request (orders), I had joined Egon and Mother in the kitchen to 'discuss this little problem.'

Mother vibrated with anxious rage in the chair beside mine. Much to Father's annoyance, Egon had taken point at the head of the table. The rest of our guests were scattered through the house, doing various bits of tracking and tracing magic. My sister Lydia simply locked herself in Father's office and got on the phone with the shipping company, who was supposed to have delivered the box of Grandmother's belongings to me after her funeral six months ago.

Sometimes the best magic was plain common sense.

"Mother called last week to ask if I'd bring a box from Grandmother's to the meeting today. I said which box, and she said, 'don't be daft, you know which one.' So I put in an order for the fruitcake we got last year, the kind with the marzipan."

"Oh, that is a good one," Father chimed in. "They use whole slices of candied mandarins and—"

"And," Mother cut us off, her voice somewhere between shrill and exhausted, "you didn't think it odd I was so insistent on you bringing a fruitcake to the council meeting? A *fruitcake*, Whitaker? Really?"

I held up my hands, staving off anything she might decide to send my way. "You're always fussy about what you serve guests, and you always order your holiday cakes from Grandmother's Bakery over on Fortnam, so, yes, fruitcake! Why would I think you meant anything else, seeing as how I never received anything from Grandmother Frost's estate? Well, anything magical, I mean," I corrected. Though not a single one of us needed help, Grandmother had made sure all of her family members were taken care of financially.

Egon steepled his spidery fingers and pressed them against the thin line of his lips. "And without these bells, the ritual will not be completed." Not a question; a flat statement of fact. The bells were an essential part of the ritual Witches performed every Winter Solstice. They were ancient and their resonance enhanced our magic, allowing us to summon forth the Wellspring from which we'd replenish our magic for another year.

We wouldn't be powerless without it—we were Witches, not battery-operated toys. But if we couldn't renew, we'd be less-than. We'd be hollow shells of ourselves.

And the bells were vital to the ritual.

"That is... complicated," Father said. "The main part of the ritual, the welcoming of the Solstice and the renewal of the magical lines of protection, can still be done. Without the bells, though, we won't be able to open the Wellspring."

Mother choked out a frantic bird cry of a sob. "If we can't access the Wellspring, our magic will diminish."

Closing my eyes, I leaned back. The headache threatening behind my left eye for the past hour crested into a mother of a migraine. "And thanks to our power-hungry ancestor Horace Frost, without the bells, all of the Witch clans will be cut off from renewing their magic for the next year."

"Don't speak ill of the dead," Mother sniffed. "He did what he had to do."

Egon gestured for us to be quiet and motioned for the tall, rangy Witch in the kitchen doorway to come forward. "Have you had any success?"

He shook his head. "We've tried various tracking spells, traceries, everything we could possibly do here." He raked his fingers through his already wild red hair and shook his head again. "Wherever the bells are, however they were sent, it's hidden from us."

Egon waved him away. The Witch hesitated but, at a sharp look from our leader, darted out of the kitchen. "Few things in this world can hide Witch magic from other Witches."

No one spoke for several long moments. We all knew the answer.

Demons.

Lydia's loud crow of laughter broke the tense silence. She bounded into the kitchen, all bright pink and green like a misplaced bit of springtime in the family tree. "You guys are gonna love this. So, the box that was supposed to go to Whitaker after all the ceremonies and shit for Grandma's funeral? It got mislabeled, apparently. A bunch of stuff was intended for one of Grandma's old friends, so it got sent with the old altar cloths and shit." She waved a piece of paper between two fingers, her grin damn near malicious in its glee. "You're gonna flip your lids, I swear. I was able to give a little Charm over the phone, and the guy spilled his guts. The box was sent to... Hey, can I get a drumroll or something?"

"Lydia," Father warned.

"Ugh, fine. The box was sent to Heliotrope's Curiosities and Antiques, care of Heliotrope Hebert."

The name sent a sharp shock of recognition through my chest, awakening a warm flush of memory, making my skin feel too tight and hot.

She dropped the paper on the table between Mother and me. "Problem is, Heliotrope Hebert's been dead for like two years now, and Grandma apparently forgot to tell her lawyer to update her will. Heliotrope's grandson got it." Her glittering, schadenfreude-laden gaze landed on me. "I think you'll remember him, Whit. The grandson running the antique shop is Rowan Hebert."

Mother groaned. "That's the...the..."

"Man?" I suggested helpfully.

"Demon-spawn," she spat. "That's the one you were interacting with at the summer Solstice council meeting. That's the Demon-spawn your grandmother made sure to invite to the meetings! He came to the Equinox, too," she added shrilly. "He brought potato salad! With *mayonnaise*." Judging by her tone, that was almost worse than his Demon heritage.

I wouldn't have put it past my mother to make actual smoke pour from her ears like a cartoon character if she'd gone on any longer. Egon, who had been dealing with her tantrums for longer than I'd been alive, cut her a sharp and quelling look. She pressed her lips into a thin line, her own volition and not Egon's magic making her silent. Though she waved us on, her glare told me I was going to hear all her opinions later.

"I remember Heliotrope Hebert," Egon said thoughtfully. "I met her grandsons a few times over the years. Rowan's presence at the past several meetings has been...diverting."

I felt the weight of his look like a tangible thing. I hadn't been the only one who'd noticed how Rowan looked at me, even though I'd brushed off the Witches who pointed it out and suggested seduce him into backing off, withdrawing the Demonborn from any attempts to become full-fledged members of the council. *If they'd had any idea what we'd gotten up to...* "I know it's an unpopular opinion, but the Demonborn *do* have a legitimate claim to a place on the council."

My mother's muffled shriek of outrage made Lydia roll her eyes. "He's not wrong," Lydia sighed. "Seriously, people."

"My own children," Mother seethed, slapping the tabletop. "Working against the clan, against their own family!"

"Nanette," Egon soothed, though his tone held a sharp edge. Mother dropped back in her chair petulantly. Father put himself between her and Egon, one hand on Mother's shoulder, and the other flexed at his side. Not for the first time, I thought my father would dearly love to punch the Witch council leader in the throat. Probably multiple times. "The entire purpose of the Grand Council is to come to a consensus on things like this." Egon reached past my father to lay his hand on my mother's, giving her knotted fingers and smiled a syrupy smile.

Once my dad was done throat punching him, I thought I might like a go.

"Now," Egon said, waving at the Wyrd sister lurking in the kitchen doorway, "Heliotrope's Antiques is in Houston, correct?"

Lydia nodded. "Yep. I already booked him a flight and a hotel." She batted her eyes at me in faux innocence. "I'm not familiar with the area, so I hope the one I picked isn't too far from Rowan's store. I mean, I guess you could always stay with him if it is."

Some days, I dearly wished we really could turn people into newts.

MOTHER MANAGED TO WITHHOLD her acidic opinions until I was waiting for the Uber to the airport. (I didn't care how much money was in my account; I wasn't going to spend it on extortionate airport parking rates.) "It would be better if you let the Witch council handle this character." As the winter wind bit sharply, she curled her arms over her middle. Flurries of snow whirled up around the porch, dancing when I gave them a little mental shove. Mother glared at a particularly large snow-nado I sent spiraling down the drive. "Whitaker, really. How childish."

I sighed. "Mother, I'm sure it was a plain old accident. There's no reason Rowan Hebert would have engaged in some baroque plot to steal the bells so we couldn't hold the Solstice ritual."

I had tried earlier to explain to her how ridiculous that idea was, but she was having none of it. She just rolled her eyes and stormed to her private suite, where she stayed for the duration of the time it took me to pack and change my hotel reservation because, of course, Lydia picked one a maximum distance from the shop, like she didn't understand how Google Maps worked.

Mother lurked in silence, no doubt gathering her best and most vitriolic arguments into a neat bouquet for my send-off.

"Demonborn hate Witches. And attacking us like this, at the Winter Solstice of all times..." She affected a dainty sob, one she had used for years to get her way before I realized what a ploy it was. When I didn't reply, she scowled. "This Hebert has it out for us, Whitaker. Mark my words. He's been lurking around, waiting for the perfect opening!"

I bit my own tongue hard, keeping back the ribald comment I *wanted* to make in response to that perfect line.

A blue sedan pulled up our long gravel drive. I'd never been so relieved to see a moderately priced older model Chevy in my life. "I'll be back by the twentieth," I promised, bending so she could brush a cool kiss to my cheek. "Mother, seriously. It's not a sinister plot."

Frowning, she folded her arms again. "Check in when you arrive, so I know he hasn't murdered you to harvest your blood for potions."

I slung my carry-on into the back seat and climbed in front with the driver. "Did she just—?"

I nodded. "Moms, right?"

"Mine just tells me to have a good trip."

I smiled and pulled out my phone, pretending to send text messages until the driver stopped trying to talk to me for the duration of the hour drive to the airport. I felt shaky and hot all over, not so much nervous as excited, I decided. Excited and anxious and okay, yes, nervous.

Would Rowan even want to speak to me after so long? I'd wanted to reach out to him but had stopped myself so many times. It's not like he was hiding away on a mountaintop somewhere. His contact info was easy to find, so I didn't have an excuse. I had to admit I'd been afraid. Afraid of what would happen if we pursued what was between us, afraid of what would happen to him if the rest of the clans made an example of someone, doing worse than saying some hateful things at a meet and greet.

Sometime in the months after the Solstice, though, that fear had turned into shame and guilt. We had chemistry, definite literal sparks flying between us when we jerked each other off at the Summer Solstice and again when we kissed at the Equinox. Then I'd just let it go.

After we'd parted ways, I'd let myself get dragged into a conference with Egon and some of the other elders, and he'd simply...left. I'd wanted to go to him, tell him we could do it again. Tell him I wanted to, I don't know, take him for coffee or something. Tell him that despite the distance, I wanted to see him more. But I was a coward, and I'd let him go. Now, with each minute bringing me closer to seeing him again, I didn't know which I felt more keenly: the sharp, needful anticipation of seeing him again or the embarrassment at how I'd treated him before.

CHAPTER THREE

Let it snow, let it snow, let it... well. You get the idea.

ROWAN

On our walk from the coffee shop to my shop, my brother Alastor squinted up at the sky and frowned. "This is your doing, isn't it?" We'd stopped on the sidewalk a few doors down from my shop, conveniently next door to his law office in one of the old Victorians that still loomed in the Montrose district of Houston. I grinned up at the sky and didn't say anything, but he knew. Snorting, he shook his head. "I don't understand how you can be so cavalier with your powers." Thick, fat, fluffy clumps fell from the sky, though they didn't stick long at all. The concrete was too warm, despite it being nominally winter in southeast Texas, and the flurries would melt nearly as soon as they hit except for some lucky, shadowy spots where they could linger at least a few hours before getting ground into the dirt and melting away. It made the entire season feel more *right.* I'd never admit it to anyone—not even my brothers—but I loved it when winter felt like *possibilities.* More than Midsummer did, the Winter Solstice always felt like a new start to me, like a time of change.

Not gonna lie—I kind of loved it.

"Winter should be cold," I said loftily. "And have at least a tiny bit of snow. No one should wear short sleeves in December. At least not in the northern hemisphere. Sweating while walking from your car to the store should be unheard of between Halloween and oh, let's say, Valentine's Day.

And if winter needed a bit of magic to be, you know, actually winter and not Spring II: Electric Boogaloo, then so be it.

Alastor shook his head. Despite only a few years between us, he definitely came off as a father-figure sometimes.

Okay, all of the time. At least when it came to things like the appropriate uses of magic.

"Seriously," I asked, poking him in the ribs with one of my fingers. A nice, sharp, brotherly jab. "We're disgustingly powerful eldritch beings. Why not use a little of that power to make it a little seasonal?" At least in a four-block radius. I might be strong, magic-wise, but I wasn't strong enough for the entire city to get flurries.

"Seriously, Rowan, you're gonna get yourself killed."

"By whom?" I demanded. "The tribunal?"

At that word, Alastor winced. It was involuntary—I could tell by the way he wouldn't look me in the eye after. He hated to show weakness, especially given his line of work. Not only was he an attorney for humans, he worked with Demonborn as well, and the occasional Fae or rare Witch who needed legal assistance from someone they didn't necessarily have to hide their nature from. "The tribunal might not support summary execution for demons engaging in high-risk behaviors that would get us caught out by humans anymore, but out of thirteen members on the tribunal, a solid seven are anti-Revelation. Seven, Rowan. That's seven ancient, powerful beings who could see to it you meet with a little accident and no one will be able to do a damned thing about it."

"Whoa, whoa. Okay. It's just a little snow." I gave my fingers a flick, sending a tiny flurry directly at his head, where it melted in a quick puff of steam. He might not like to use his magic as much as I did, but he definitely had it, and was definitely powerful. Well, unless we're talking about sigils then he was so, so, sloppy. It was a disappointment to our father, who was known for his intricate and fantastic sigilwork.

Though, to be fair, Father had been disappointed in all of our sigil work and the fact I refused to use sigils to travel between places angered him no-end. *Sigils are a time-honored Demonborn tradition, Rowan! No one gets travelsickness from sigil-travel! You're making that up!*

Spoiler: I wasn't. And if you think getting nauseated on a car trip is bad, try it while moving between dimensions.

Super gross.

"It's not just a little snow," Alastor sighed, raking his fingers through his dark hair and setting it into disarray—he'd fix it before he saw his first client of the day, I was sure, but the thought of him going into work looking a bit disheveled amused me in a little brother way so I kept my mouth shut. "It's the fact we're on the precipice of this whole Revelation crisis and we," he gestured between us, but I knew he meant all of Demonkind. "We're not truly part of it, yet you're doing your best to keep us on the Council's radar. This," he nodded at the flurries, "this is going to piss off the wrong people if you get caught."

"And how would I get caught?" I sighed. "It's a tiny bit of weather magic. We learn this stuff in preschool, Alastor. Come on now. Aren't you being more paranoid than usual?"

He glanced at his smart watch and scowled, though I wasn't sure if it was at the time or me. "Two days ago, Rickson Blair stopped by my office for a chat," he said in a low whisper.

Okay, now I was a tiny bit unnerved. Rickson Blair was a tribunal member, an old friend of Father's, and possibly one of the oldest Demons on Earth. And about as pleasant and kind as a lion with a thorn in his paw. "What did he want?"

"To chat. And to remind me that I'm nominally the head of the family now that Father's gone and I should remind my baby brother that, no matter what side of the Council Demonkind ends up falling on, there will be humans who want us destroyed. And no amount of politicking can stop that."

Behind me, the door to my shop jingled as Chloe let herself in to start the day. Alastor glanced at his own office and made a half-step towards it, ready to get to his own work and, most importantly, away from our conversation. "Blair is very wrong," I finally said. "When it comes time, there's going to be humans who support us. Not just us, but the others as well. Witches, Fae—"

"Do you honestly believe that?"

I nodded. "I have to, Alastor. If we don't push to be part of the Revelation itself, we'll be out in the cold and you know historically how we've been portrayed. Outsiders, not wanting to be part of the larger community..."

He sighed. "And it's been part of the reason why we're vilified, I know but—"

"But," I said, giving him another poke, "I want you to think about helping." The idea wasn't a new one—I'd been toying with it for a while. I just hadn't planned on bringing it up so soon. Originally, I'd been hoping to ask Alastor after the Solstice but it felt like time was shorter than I'd thought so the words rushed out before I could stop them. "You work with humans day in and day out, Alastor. You can help steer the Council in the right direction when it comes to dealing with the humans in ways that Simon can't."

"Simon's human," he bristled. He was oddly protective of our brother Ellery's mostly-human boyfriend. Simon was human by birth but had been raised in Sidhe as a changeling for longer than a normal human lifespan before being kicked out as the Sidhe started to polish up their image in preparation for the big R.

I said as much to Alastor as we started walking the last dozen or so yards towards our respective businesses. "And," I cut him off, "I just want you to think about it, okay? There's not much we can do about the demons who are against the idea, but if we can get some sort of solid plan in place—"

"You're far too optimistic about this," Alastor muttered, turning to head up the narrow flagstone walk to his practice's front door.

"That's not a no."

"That's a fuck off, we'll talk later."

I grinned to myself, the churning in my gut calming a tiny bit. Ducking into my shop, I shook off my scarf and tucked my thin gloves into my jacket pocket. "Morning!"

Chloe, my cousin and sometimes shop assistant, rolled her eyes, ducking back behind the counter as the door chimed. "I know this is you," she muttered, pointing at the wet sidewalk outside. "I'm *not* dreaming of a muddy Solstice."

I offered a cheery smile at the customer tottering in under the weight of a dirty, misshapen box and left Chloe to deal with whatever they were trying to sell on consignment. The outlay of magic required to make it snow even a tiny bit was taxing, and I wanted—no, needed—a nap. It was entirely worth it, though, when I flipped on the light in my office and saw the icy frost limning the window and felt the cold bite of winter air seeping in around the poorly pointed edges.

The message light on my desk phone was blinking, and I knew, without looking, I'd have several emails to answer, but lethargy rimed my bones. I curled myself onto the old, unsaleable settee taking up one corner of my office, barely remembering to tug my grandmother's afghan over my legs before I fell into a deep, velvety sleep.

For ten minutes.

"Ro!" Chloe's strident cry dragged me out of my near-nap. "Ro, you need to come up here a sec!"

"I really don't," I muttered into the stiff brocade of the sofa. A few seconds later, Chloe knocked on my office door. "Seriously, I'm taking my lunch," I called. "I'll be out in...what? Twenty minutes. Ish."

"Rowan, I need you out here now," she hissed through the closed door. "Do not make me open this!"

I groaned. Would using my powers for evil really be bad? I wouldn't be the first Demonborn to do it. Others had for far less than being denied a nap. "Fine, fine. Just a sec."

"Meet me at the counter. Like, now."

I flung the afghan off my body, half-tempted to drag it behind me like a petulant child. Giving in to temptation, I pulled it along behind me. My exertion earlier had left me chilled to the bone, and something else crept along the edges of my awareness, prodding at my defenses and making me feel exposed. I tugged my grandmother's blanket over my shoulders and padded to the office door, letting the charms Grammy wove into the design settle over me and chase away a chill that had nothing to do with the weather.

I hesitated before easing out into the shop proper. I doubted there'd be many customers, if any, given the snowmageddon going on, but at the same time, even if there were, hopefully they'd see me warding off the creeping chill in the shop, not a grown man who needed his blankie.

My office was in the farthest back corner, the door hidden between tall racks of carnival glass and box sets of out-of-date encyclopedias. From the front of the shop, it was difficult, if not impossible, to see. The location gave me the perfect opportunity to check out whatever crisis Chloe thought she had a few times per week, whenever she panic-knocked on my door and insisted I get up to the front desk. Usually, it was the register being out of tape or a customer haggling over a price.

Clutching the afghan around me like a cloak, I hesitated in my office doorway, an unpleasant Something churning in my belly. "Is this about the delivery from the Benjamin estate?" I asked, shuffling out into the showroom. "You can give it to me straight, Clo. They used the auction house's shipping team, didn't they? Even after I told them not to." I groaned, ducking around a precariously stuffed bookshelf full of cookbooks from churches and ladies' circles circa 1920-1929. "That was a box of delicate uranium glass and I swear, if those lunkheads shattered it..."

"It's not the uranium glass," she said sharply. "Christ, how slow can you walk?"

When I was able to make it snow a little, I'd had such high hopes for the day I'd had a sliver of relief when it hadn't immediately turned to a rain of frogs or a become unseasonably warm instead. I thought maybe, maybe this day would be one of the ones where something only a tiny bit annoying happened. Like I ran out of correction fluid or dropped one of the milk glass vases I'd been trying to shift for months.

But no.

Apparently, that funny feeling wasn't a premonition about shattered, rare glass or some cash register related drama. It was Whitaker Frost in my shop. Whitaker Frost dressed to the nines in a designer sweater and these gray slacks that did *amazing* things for his ass. Which was already pretty damn amazing, so you can figure just how weak in the knees the sight made me.

Shit, shit, shit! I tugged the blanket closer, but the warm tingle of Heliotrope's magic did very little to soothe the wave of *what the fuck* swamping my mental boat. A pulse of lust pushed through me, dredging the never-far-away memory of the way his mouth felt on mine, his hand on my cock as we gasped and breathed one another in, how his body arched and shuddered against me, the gasp and breathless laugh when I licked his spend off my fingers, holding his gaze with mine. On its heels, though, came suspicion.

I haven't heard from him in over six months, and now he's in my shop. Hell, I wasn't expecting flowers and a ring, but a 'hey how are you, thanks for the handy' text would've been nice... Oh, who was I kidding? I would have definitely been down for flowers. And dirty weekends when we could get time away from our jobs. And late-night calls. Or early morning. Or mid-afternoon. Or... Well.

Between his easy dismissal of me and the rumblings about Demonborn still coming from the Witches and the Grand Council itself, seeing Whitaker just feet away from me left me in a tangle of excitement mixed with trepidation.

"I just need to speak with Rowan Hebert," he said to Chloe. She stared up at his towering figure with a decidedly unimpressed look on her face. "Please," he added through gritted teeth.

"Rowan's really busy," she said flatly. The tiny tendrils of her magic sought me out, familiar warmth brushing my cheek when she found me hiding behind the tall shelf full of carnival glassware. "I can let him know you stopped by, though, if you want to leave your name and contact information. Are you looking for something in particular? I mean, I'm not the expert he is, but I know some stuff."

Whitaker closed his eyes. I could see his jaw tic from where I stood. I didn't have Chloe's skill with Shielding or Seeking, but I was damned good at not being seen. People ignored me even if I didn't give them a little mental push. Whitaker had been different, though.

Or so I thought.

If you consider mutual hand jobs in the bathroom while some weird dude named Egon droned on and on about the history of Witch clans and how they were all 'true Witches'—yeah, trust me, I didn't miss that dig at me and mine—different. When the Witch king or whoever he was hit the one-hour mark in his oral history of how awesome non-Demons were, I slipped away to the men's room, only vaguely fantasizing about Whitaker following me. In fact, when he stepped in while I washed my hands, locking the door behind him, I thought maybe I'd fallen asleep out of boredom and was having a really amazing dream.

One frantic, sloppy, knee-shaking, spine-melting handjob later, and I was a freaking goner. He slipped out after a quick hand wash and a shaky, sideways smile. I followed a few minutes later, just in time to see him take up his spot at the head of the table like nothing had happened.

Too many eyes turned to track my progress across the room for me to trail after him like the dick-matized goner that I was. Therefore, I took a seat near one of the Unseelie reps to the council and pretended to be absolutely enthralled by the lengthy reading of the potluck roster for the upcoming autumnal Equinox meeting.

When Madam Frost died a few weeks after that, I asked my brother Ellery to go to the memorial and funeral rituals as the representative of the Demonborn. Losing Madame Frost had been like losing Grandmother all over again and I hadn't been able to face both my grief and the aggressive anti-Demon sentiment present amongst the other guests at the same time. I must have looked terrible because he'd agreed without a fuss.

"I feel like you're not really getting the gravity of the situation," Whitaker said in a low voice that did *things* to me. Things I had no business experiencing in front of my cousin. "I'm not here as a customer, but as...as..."

"If you're not going to buy anything, you have to leave," Chloe said. "Sorry, but if you're looking for a place to, like, hang out and chill, there's From the Ground Up down the street or the library or something."

Whitaker dropped his chin and closed his eyes, fingers tapping out an agitated rhythm on the polished wood countertop. Finally, he exhaled noisily and opened his eyes. "Right. Fine. Are you a clerk, or do you manage this place?"

"I'm Rowan's assistant." She narrowed her eyes. "Why?"

"I'm looking for a box that was sent here by mistake, sometime after the Autumnal Equinox, and don't give me that look. I know you know very well when that was. The box was from the estate of Lucinda Frost and contained silver bells, very old and delicate. They weren't meant to come here, and, frankly, we have no idea how the mistake even occurred, but I need them back. Or," he added, his voice faltering ever so slightly, "I need to know who's bought them if they've been sold already. It's...it's vital."

Chloe shook her head. "Sorry, I don't know about any of the shipments Rowan gets." She glanced at me again.

Ugh. Fine. "I'm sorry," I said, pushing myself forward. "I was in the middle of a meeting."

Whitaker turned on his heel and faced me, a look I couldn't decipher sliding over his features before he gave me a stiff smile, nothing like the sweet, adorkable, sexy one he'd shown me at either of our previous encounters. "A meeting with...the Sandman?" He gestured to the blanket over my shoulders.

Shit. "It's colder than I expected."

He hummed thoughtfully. "Yeah, I noticed the sudden snowfall. Pretty unusual for the area. Downright *magical.* I was actually under the impression Demonborn magic wasn't powerful enough for something like that." He indicated the fat flakes still tumbling down outside. "Not without help."

The door swung open, and Mrs. Ellis trudged in, bearing a box of old romance novels she knew damn well I wasn't going to touch. I tilted my head in the direction of my office, signaling Whitaker should follow me. "Chloe, please help Mrs. Ellis," I said pleasantly. "The number for the library's resale shop is by the phone." I held my office door open for Whitaker, following him in. After the briefest hesitation, I locked it behind me. "Mrs. Ellis is in at least twice a week, trying to offload old books she digs out of her mother-in-law's storage unit or picks up at garage sales."

"Why don't you tell her to stop?"

I shrugged. "She's lonely. She's bored. She spends an hour bothering Chloe or talking to me about her mother's different collections. Then she goes on about her day feeling like she's done something. We send the books on to the library's resale shop, where they no doubt end up reselling at least half of them to Mrs. Ellis. Rinse and repeat."

"That's...awfully kind," he said after a pause in which his face seemed unable to decide what expression to make. He settled on a smile making me feel the tiniest bit warmer inside.

"Being kind is free," I said, parroting one of Chloe's favorite sayings. "Mrs. Ellis needs some kindness in her life. We all do."

And there went the smile. "Is that why you accepted my grandmother's invitation to the council meetings? To be kind to an old lady?"

Here we go. "No. I accepted because I was invited, and it's been over a century since a Demonborn was party to any council votes. Our invitations kept getting lost in the mail, apparently."

"The meetings are open to all non-humans who—"

"All non-humans who aren't Demonborn. We've heard it for centuries, you know. If I recall my history correctly, your own great-great-great-grandfather was the one to officially ban Demonborn at any and all council meetings. Though that ban didn't last terribly long, at least not in an official sense." I showed him my teeth in a parody of a smile, waiting for the explosion or at least a bit of seething snark. It happened every time I'd approached a council member about putting my name forward as a representative. The insults, the half-truths, the downright *wrongness* of their attitude towards Demonborn. As if they didn't know that, without us, there would be no magic in the first place.

Whitaker leaned back in the creaky leatherette chair and steepled his fingers on his flat stomach, regarding me coolly. "And my grandmother felt you should be there. Despite everything."

"Yes. She was very encouraging and brought up several very compelling arguments for my presence at the meetings."

The butterflies in my stomach brought friends, and they'd all been drinking Red Bull and snorting Pixy Sticks. I didn't want to tell him she didn't have to work *that* hard to get me to attend and that my intentions weren't one hundred percent altruistic. My face felt warm. The heat spread down my throat and up to my ears, leaving me a color

I just knew was not only unflattering but extremely telling. Whitaker, bless his heart, pretended not to notice even though I saw his eyes widen a fraction before he feigned interest in my snow globe.

"So, I'm assuming you're not here simply to discuss my attendance at the upcoming Solstice meeting, even though my invitation has once again been lost in the mail because Madam Frost is no longer with us?" I supposed I should have felt a smidge guilty for invoking her name simply to be catty, but really I think it's what she would have wanted.

It was Whitaker's turn to blush, and he did it beautifully, sending my thoughts skittering towards memories of what he looked like at his crisis point, mere moments before orgasm. "Ah, unfortunately, while it is to do with the Solstice, I'm not here to request your presence. Um. Specifically."

Ouch. "Generally, then?"

He fondled my snow globe. Which...yeah, dirty thoughts. I was definitely on Santa's naughty list.

Seriously, he told me himself. But this would further cement things.

"When my grandmother passed after the Equinox, things were a bit chaotic with the dividing of her estate. She had a will but apparently didn't keep it up as well as she could have." He set the globe back down and fidgeted with his hair, smoothed his waistcoat (unf, waistcoat), and sighed. "Something meant to go to me was accidentally sent to you. Well, more specifically, your grandmother."

"My grandmother died two years ago." I made a face. "Is this some Witch thing? Sending bequests to the dead?" Seriously, and they thought we were strange.

"What? No. I mean, not for us anyway. The Gores might, but they're an odd family anyway." He waved off the ramble with one hand, shaking his head like he was knocking out the wandering thoughts. "A box. Containing silver bells. It was a family heirloom and somehow got sent to your grandmother instead of...well, family."

My grandmother Heliotrope had never mentioned even knowing Madam Frost, much less knowing her well enough to be sent a package from the woman's estate. (Yes, yes, Heliotrope, Rowan, my mother Rose, my brother Douglas—like the fir, but he steadfastly went by his middle name Alastor, as did my brother Damson, who insisted on going by his middle name Ellery. We all had a theme going on with the names) "Are you certain?"

He produced a slip of paper with tracking numbers and the store's address, my name, and a few lines of chicken scratch that looked like a hotel name and room number. "Sorry, my sister's handwriting is worse than mine. It's the information from the shipping company that was supposed to send me the box. Lydia—that's my sister—convinced them to give us the information."

"Convinced or," I wiggled my fingers in an *oooooh, magic* gesture, "convinced?"

He snorted. "Probably more of the latter than I'm comfortable admitting, but Lydia's very good at talking people around to her way of seeing things. Though that might also be a bit," he made the same gesture I had. "I'm never sure with her."

"You said this was sent after the Equinox? Do you know how? Like overnight, express, ground...?" I glanced up at him to find a bemused expression on his face. "That's a no. Okay, let me see what I can find here." I brought up the Ship-Us website and dug around until I found their well-hidden tracking option and wrangled with it until I found a package from Lucinda Frost to Heliotrope Hebert, shipped from Bellerive, Maine and arriving in Houston, Texas in early October. "No signature requested, so I have no idea who signed for it or if it was accepted at all. We've had some bad luck with packages going missing when a delivery person decides to leave them on the front step instead of using the office entrance around back or ringing my apartment doorbell upstairs." I sighed. "Shit."

"Shit," he echoed sadly. "Is there a chance they might be in your stockroom or something?"

He sounded hopeful, and I hated to burst his bubble, but I had to tell the truth. "I don't have a stockroom. What you see out there is what you get. I sell antiques and curiosities, so it's not like I have bulk lots of hurricane lamps or a gross of rolltop desks out back in case we run short on the floor."

"And there's no chance your assistant out there might know anything?"

"I'm guessing these bells are more than a family heirloom?"

"They are...community property, in a sense."

"Ah? A Witch thing?"

"Something like that, yes." Darting a glance towards my office door, he shifted uncomfortably. "There's not really a good way for me to ask this, so I'll come right out and do it."

"I do appreciate forthright men," I murmured, leaning back in my chair.

"There are some rumors you sell certain items to non-humans. Under the radar, as it were."

Fucking Hell.

"I once sold some old Bon Jovi tour merch to a loup-garou in a cash sale at a flea market and may have forgotten to put the money in my till, but in my defense, I was eighteen and stupid." Heliotrope's little side business had not been very secret, but it was treated as one of those *we'll pretend we're not coming to a Demonborn for ritual supplies and magical items, and she'll pretend she never saw us if anyone asks* situations. A poorly kept open secret.

Raising his dark brows, Whitaker gave me one of those *you've got to be shitting me* looks. "Right. My grandmother's services. You want to know if I've kept them up. Well. Yes and no. They're available, but so far, the only person who's asked for anything has been Chloe's sister Marigold, and I told her no because she was fifteen and addled. We don't *do* love spells," I added at his questioning look. "Taking away someone's free will? No Demonborn worth knowing would." And, as a rule, we weren't very good at spells. Not like Witches had become. We excelled at sigils and incantations, at manipulating nature to an extent, tweaking reality, and could start truly excellent campfires.

If we had to lean into a stereotype, being fire-resistant and pyroamorous was not the worst we could have picked.

"And ones not worth knowing?"

"Well, answered your own question there, didn't you? Come on. I'll show you Heliotrope's secret stash so you can assure whoever is spreading those rumors that she was—and I am—on the up and up." Without letting myself think too hard about where I was taking Whitaker, I led him from my office and told Chloe we were going up to my apartment for a few minutes, and she was in charge of the shop.

Her mouth popped open in an O of surprise and not a little curious, gossipy interest, but she schooled her face back into a customer-service smile and nodded. "Sure thing, Ro."

"Did she wink at me?" Whitaker asked as we stepped out into the wintry air outside.

The snow was falling slower now, still sticking, and a news van was stationed down at the end of the street, where the kids on homemade sleds were now showing off tricks on someone's sloping front lawn. Gotta love a lack of zoning laws, putting shops right next to old Victorian town homes, gas stations besides daycares. Houston was a mess, but I kind of loved it sometimes.

"Probably," I told Whitaker. "She thinks you're cute."

"Ah. Well. Not my type. As you know."

"Do I?" I led him around the side of the shop into the narrow space between Heliotrope's and a law firm in one of those old Victorians, owned by my dear brother as luck would have it. When Ellery glanced out his office window and saw I was leading a man up to my apartment over the shop, I waved and pretended not to notice his double-take. He didn't have much room to talk. I knew for a fact his human boy-toy was curled up napping in his office most afternoons.

As I trotted up the narrow metal steps to my apartment door, I was keenly aware of Whitaker barely a few feet behind me, how he waited on the rickety stairs as I perched on the rusty landing, jiggling and shouldering the door until it popped open for us. "It's not as bad inside," I promised.

"It's not terrible outside. It's charming."

"That's real estate agent speak for 'old and probably a death trap,'" I laughed, waving him in ahead of me. His low whistle of surprise made me grin. "See?"

"This is amazing," he said softly. "Did you do this yourself?"

"I had help from Chloe." My apartment was tiny, all things considered. While the footprint took up about half the size of the shop downstairs, a large storage closet took up most of the space. What I did have, however, I wanted to make beautiful. The walls were painted with murals depicting the four seasons transitioning one into the other, blending as one wall met the next. Where windows and doors broke up the murals, Chloe and I had made faux columns out of plaster and chicken wire. On close inspection, it wasn't exactly high art, but it made my little apartment with shitty air conditioning in summer and nearly nil heating on the three cold days we got per year feel like some ancient temple. My small altar space was in the tiny hearth, which hadn't been lit once since I moved in ten years before, on my eighteenth birthday. Instead, I used it for my own sacred space.

Whitaker paused in front of it, bending down to see my Solstice altar already set up even though it was over a week until the day.

"I was wondering," he said, straightening when he realized I was staring at him staring at my things. "I mean, if you practiced something...traditional."

"Are you one of those Witches that think Demons are all horns and fire?"

He followed me to the storage closet door, hidden between two columns draped with fake ivy and, in deference to its spot on the summer wall, cascading flowers. "No, but I didn't want to assume."

A funny little quiggle danced through my belly, making my heart flutter with a misplaced butterfly. He was looking around my space so intently I felt exposed. Worse than naked. Unlocking the closet door, I pushed it wide. "Here we are," I said. "Heliotrope Hebert's secret stash. Now mine."

"Holy shit, Rowan," he breathed, stepping into the brightly lit closet. It ran the length of the store below and was nine feet across. The walls were lined with shelves, while several long tables were lined up down the center, bundles of herbs and bottles of oils and tinctures and whatnot in progress where I'd left them to steep or brew or whatever they needed to do. "From what I was told, your grandmother was selling, like, black-market crystal balls or the blood of virgins or something."

"We ran out of virgin blood some time in '17, and I just never bothered to restock."

He rolled his eyes. "Smartass."

I bit down on my knee-jerk reply, a comment about *his* ass, and instead smirked. I swear he could read my mind, though, because he turned away and bent waaaaay over to look at boxes on the lower shelves. "All that's down there are bottles and the sachets we use if someone needs herb mixes."

Disappointed, he stood back up and looked around the room once more. "Fuck."

"Hoping it was gonna be easy, huh?"

"Can't blame a guy."

"Come on, let me make you some tea, and we'll figure something out." Whitaker trailed after me like a duckling as I led him back downstairs to the shop's break room, where I kept a stash of tea.

A tall, dark, handsome, sexy duckling.

Wait. I just made it super weird.

WELL. THE TEA WASN'T in the breakroom. "Chloe? Have you seen...what's that?"

A large, shiny, white box sat on the counter, one corner bashed and crumpled, marked with a bright yellow sticker reading, "Oops! Our bad! This box has been damaged in shipping!" printed on it in acid-green. Another sticker, this one with an error code and a customer service number smudged all to hell, was pasted below it.

"This just got here," Chloe announced. "Some dude dropped it off and ran." She poked the side of the box with one of our logo pens. "It gives me the creeps. I didn't recognize the company, and he didn't say anything, just dropped it on the counter and scuttled out like he was afraid I was going to talk to him or something."

Whitaker nudged past me, a breathless little laugh on his lips. "No way."

Chloe shrugged. "Guy didn't have a name on his shirt or anything, only a red-and-black uniform. Did UPS change their colors?"

"How in the Hell..." I began, but Whitaker laughed again, this time a damn near cackle.

"Magic," he said, reaching for the box. "Magic and probably a little nudge from my sister Lydia. She called the shipping company to get them in gear, and I bet they found this stuck behind a rack somewhere." As he spoke, he fiddled the box open, tearing at the tape with no regard for the intended address. "Ha!" He tipped the open box so I could see the contents. Neatly wrapped in bubble wrap like they were merely mundane everyday items were twelve silver bells, round balls with a small hole near the top and a built-in little loop.

"Jingle bells?" I laughed. "Seriously? This whole drama has been about jingle bells? Hell, you can go to the Dollar General and get a pack of a hundred right now, and you'd have saved yourself the trouble!"

Whitaker's joyful expression dimmed. "Look closer. These aren't *jingle bells.* They're ancient. They were made by the Sidhe as a gift to my ancestors, one for each of the major clans, plus a thirteenth bell for the stranger."

Chloe leaned closer to peer at the bells. "They're shiny. What's the big deal, though? Did someone want us to sell them or something?" She reached for one near the top and drew back suddenly. "Ow! What the Hell?" A red welt shone brightly on her palm like a fresh burn. "Are those things fucking booby-trapped or something? Not cool, asshole!" Darting around the counter, she made a beeline for the bathroom. "I need cold water on this! Ow, ow, ow!"

"Chloe!" I started after her, but she waved me back. "The hell is going on?" A greasy churn of nausea roiled in my belly, making me sorely regret the cup of coffee I'd thought was good enough for breakfast. "What the Hell kind of a curse is this?" I demanded. "Is she going to be okay?" The thought of something happening to Chloe, something worse than a burn on her hand, sickened me.

Demons could heal from almost anything magical, but it wasn't pleasant. Bits of old Witch-magic, things the older ones knew, could weaken a Demon to the point we wished we were dead, keep us on that brink. The thought of Chloe going through anything close wakened the flame in me. I wanted to rip the box away from Whitaker and lay into him with claws and fire.

No, not Whitaker—Witches. The Witches who would curse something to hurt a Demon.

Gingerly, Whitaker plucked out the bell Chloe had been reaching for. It was still wrapped in plastic and looked entirely ordinary, as far as a large, ancient jingle bell made by Faeries could look ordinary. "It feels fine," he said quietly, mostly to himself. "It's not the one for the Frosts, but the magic on it isn't hurting me." He rummaged in the box, touching each one. "They're all the same. The magic is still imbued in them, but they're not warded to cause harm, should they be touched."

I reached out before he could stop me and laid one finger atop the nearest bell. Instantly, pain flared along my nerves from my fingertip to my throat, making me gasp and jerk back. It was sharp and searing, almost electric. My finger was red, already blistering. "Whitaker," I demanded, pinning him with a glare, "what the Hell is in my shop?"

CHAPTER FOUR

Pretty Packages All Tied Up with Terms and Conditions

WHITAKER

Looking tired and in desperate need of a shower, Lydia finally answered my Skype call. "There's nothing on record about the bells being under any sort of protection spell," she yawned. "That doesn't mean they aren't, though."

"The spell just affected the two Demonborn," I reminded her.

"It's possible one of our ancestors laid it on there after the whole bad blood with the Demonborn thing got messy, but I don't know why they would. Those bells are made with blood from the Witch clans and wouldn't work to draw power at the Solstice for anyone but clan members."

I nodded, squinting into space as I turned things over in my mind. "Except," I said slowly, "the stranger's bell. It was made without blood. Because it was meant to be a placeholder." A soft knock fell on the apartment door, and a moment later, Rowan stepped in, his finger bandaged and scowl not gone but at least slightly reduced. "You don't have to knock on your own door."

Lydia's smile was a curly thing. "Oh, did I pick the wrong hotel? Do you have to stay with Mr. Hebert? Aw." She snapped her fingers in exaggerated disappointment. "I'm sorry, favorite brother."

Rowan leaned over the back of the sofa to peer at my sister's face on the laptop screen. "Hello, Miss Frost. Am I correct in assuming you are the one who left a message on my office voicemail informing me that Whitaker is an asshole, but he means well, and to cut him a bit of slack?"

She beamed. "You got it! I'm so glad!"

"Jesus Christ," I muttered, the headache throbbing behind my eye and threatening to crank up the intensity. "Before I hang up on you," I said over her laughter, "there's something else. One of the bells is missing. The stranger bell."

"Oh," she said softly, eyes going round. "That's...not ideal."

"Yeah..."

Rowan leaned in again. "From what I understand, there's no specific Witch clan associated with the stranger bell, correct?"

I nodded, and Lydia said, "Wait, Whitaker told you that? Seriously?"

"Was he wrong?"

A devious glint flashed in her eyes. "Not at all. I just wanted to make sure I understood. So, Whit, you gonna tell Egon or keep it as a surprise for the Solstice?"

"Ugh."

Rowan stared at me with a raised brow.

"He *is* the head of the clan council."

"Not to be confused with the Grand Council," Lydia added, her voice tinny through the laptop speakers. "The clan council is the Witch's council. The Grand Council is...well. You know."

Rowan jerked his chin in acknowledgment. "Yeah, I'm familiar."

Sighing, Lydia looked at something off to the side. "Look, it's been hella busy here the past two days. Mom's in a lather about the meeting and has us all decorating and sprucing up, and ugh, I'm just covered in mistletoe sap, and I'm pretty sure I'm allergic to holly and ivy. What I'm trying to say is this whole thing is hella major. Like...hella."

"Hella," Rowan and I echoed solemnly. His snort of laughter made something bright and warm bubble up in my chest. I was going to have to stop thinking of it as a nebulous 'something' and admit I'd had a crush on him for months. Yes, it had been abstract, but sitting next to him? Breathing in his citrus-spice smell, feeling the buzz of magic or connection or something else between us? Yeah, it was definitely becoming actual rather than abstract.

"Ugh! Listen! What I mean is that if you come back without all of them?" She made an explosion noise with her mouth and spread her fingers apart in front of her face. "And not just Mom being pissed at you for getting a handy from a Demonborn. No offense, Mr. Hebert!"

"Your mother knows we...oh, my God," Rowan groaned, hiding his face in his hands. "That's fantastic."

"Oh, she thinks you're trying to seduce your way onto the council! Especially after that scandal with your brother and the little human dude!" Lydia laughed. Beside me, Rowan stiffened and drew in a sharp breath.

"Bye, Lydia! Talk to you later!" I shut off Skype and closed my computer. "Rowan..."

"It's fine," he muttered into his hands. "It's all fine."

It really wasn't. On pretty much any level. It was just various grades of goddammit. The top of the heap was the missing bell. Well, the missing bell and what it meant for the clans' ritual in barely over a week.

"If we don't have the bell, we can't draw on the Wellspring. Before we knew where the box had been sent, some of the clan members tried various tracking and tracing spells, but nothing worked. It was like the bells were hidden. And few things can block Witch magic..."

I didn't need to spell (ha) it out for him. Demon magic was far more ancient than even the oldest Witch magic. A strong enough Demon could easily tear apart the strongest Witch charm or spell like wet tissue paper.

"Are you saying Demon magic hid them? That's ridiculous." He shoved himself to his feet and strode into his kitchenette.

"Not to many of the Witch council members. My mother being a major one. Egon...I'm not sure."

"Your grandmother was fine with Demonborn joining the Grand Council. She," he brandished a bottle of water at me, "didn't have her head up her ass."

My head throbbed, my fingers itched to grab hold of him again, and every synapse in between fired wildly with conflicting orders. It was my turn to groan, letting my head thump not too gently against the kitchenette wall. "If we can't draw from the Wellspring, our powers diminish," I finally said. "That's why we need the bells. At Winter Solstice, we draw on the Wellspring and...and..."

He took a swig of his water. "Top off the tank?"

"That makes it sound weird. We reconnect with the ancient source of our magic and the spiritual birthplace of the Witches." I parroted back what every little Witch was taught when we first started learning how to spell. Well, learning how to make spells. Totally different thing. Though in both cases, you could really screw things up if you swapped letters around.

Grinning slightly, Rowan shook his head. "When did they stop teaching you lot about how Witches even came to be?"

"The original thirteen were blessed by the Wellspring," I began in a monotone, reciting. "They were deemed worthy vessels of the power within the Wellspring and blessed by its touch."

He set his water down on the counter and hopped up to sit beside it. "And where do y'all think this power comes from?" he asked, spreading his hands in a *give me more* gesture. "Where did this Wellspring originate?"

"It's always been there," I said slowly. "The first Witches were gifted with magic by the keeper of the Wellspring."

"Who was...?"

"Ah, the name was lost to time," I said. "This is basic knowledge, even for Demonborn, isn't it? I mean, if even the Merfolk know of the Wellspring—"

"Witches are only Witches because of Demons," he interjected, "not some mythical, benevolent Wellspring keeper who just decided tra la la, let me teach this rando how to bend the universe." His smile was barely more than a tightening of his lips, rueful and tired. "The only reason your lot hates mine is because we," he tapped himself on the chest with one finger, "made you. And your clan elders can't stand the fact they didn't spring fully formed out of some magical rock or something."

What he was saying wasn't entirely unheard of, even in the most tightly knit Witch circles. It was simply thought of a rude myth, an alternative history. Some of our scholars had considered it a possibility at one point, but it had been dismissed as unlikely. And I honestly never learned why. Rowan was staring at me with a tired, annoyed gaze, making me feel antsy. "I know that, for a long while now, Witches have been less than fond of Demonborn, but—"

"Less than fond?" Rowan asked archly. "You seemed pretty damned fond of me at the Summer Solstice."

He had an oddly expectant look on his face like he was daring me to deny it.

"You're not wrong," I admitted. "I was very fond of you then. And at the Equinox."

He took another long draught from his water bottle before setting it aside on the counter, pushing it back so he could spread his arms and sit back. "You seemed a bit fonder of me at the Solstice," he teased. "I've had several very *fond* dreams about what we did in that bathroom." He lowered his voice just a little, and he must have put just a touch of Demon magic to the words because my blood felt like it was on fire when he added, "To be honest, I'd have let you have me back at the Equinox. I'd have let you take me there on the ground behind the dining pavilion instead of just kissing."

"Oh?" My cock twitched against my thigh. "If I'd known..."

"I figured you wanted the thrill of a dirty little secret."

The kitchenette was not anywhere near large enough to pretend I was keeping my distance. As he watched me warily, I took a few steps forward, stopping just before I bumped into his knees. "Not every Witch hates Demons," I said quietly. "My grandmother didn't. My sister doesn't. I don't."

He watched me for several heartbeats before he reached up with his right hand and brushed a lock of my hair off my forehead. "I didn't go with the intent to try and seduce someone," he said urgently, softly. "It crossed my mind, when I saw you at the Equinox, that maybe you thought..."

"No," I promised. "I never thought you were trying something. Well, nothing I didn't want anyway."

He smiled, deep dimples popping at the corners of his mouth. He glanced up at me from under dark, thick lashes, worrying his lower lip before he spoke again. "What you were saying earlier, about the Wellspring? When I said if it weren't for Demons..."

"Our sacred texts do not record the name of the first Witches, only that they were gifted magic by the keeper of the Wellspring. The spring was opened at the Winter Solstice, during the long darkness, as a gift to those first Witches. It's generally believed the keeper of the Wellspring was a Sidhe or perhaps a powerful nature spirit."

"And you believe every one of your sacred texts when it comes to Demons?"

I shook my head slowly. "If I did, I definitely wouldn't want to kiss you right now."

Tipping his head back, Rowan considered me for the longest time. "Before I let you kiss me, I want you to make me a promise."

"Am I about to make a deal with a devil?" I teased gently, making him roll his eyes and huff.

"Yes, but instead of your soul, I'm asking for your Word."

The capital letter was inherent. "My Word. That's...that's pretty damn serious, Rowan."

He nodded slowly. "I'm about to ask you for something you're likely to talk yourself out of unless I pin you to it."

"I'm not sure whether I should be aroused or scared or both."

His smile was beautiful, crinkling his eyes and deepening those dimples again. "Well, we can definitely discuss the *both* option if that's something you're into, but not now. We need to know each other a little better before I bring out my flogger."

"Your *what*?"

"So, do I have your Word?" he asked, ignoring my squawk.

I hesitated just a moment more. Whatever he was going to ask, I had a feeling it wouldn't be something beyond my reach; it wouldn't be something to hurt me or shame me. I finally, slowly, nodded.

"Okay. I'll find your stranger bell, and you let me bring the bells to the council and present my case for Demonkind being included. We go before the Solstice, and, after hearing me fair, if the answer is no, I step back. I don't interfere. I wait a year and a day to ask again."

The room shifted wildly for a moment, a pulse of magic moving through it, through us. Magic that didn't feel like my own and, judging by the look on Rowan's face, wasn't his either. As quickly as it had started, it was over. "I think my Word was just accepted..."

Rowan nodded, rubbing his palms on his trousers. "You were saying something about a kiss a few moments ago?"

"Was I? Weird. I don't remember that." He scowled impatiently when I laughed, leaning in those last few inches to bring our faces closer together. "Maybe you can refresh my memory."

Rowan smelled like oranges and cloves and incense and red wine. I was drunk on him just from breathing in his scent. He stared up at me with wide, unblinking eyes. Not scared, just wary. Waiting.

"I'm sorry about the Summer Solstice."

"Are you?" He pulled away, as much as he could with the wall at his back and me at his front. "I thought—"

"Fuck! I mean I'm sorry about disappearing on you." I reached for him again, slowly so he could have time to rebuff me or move away. When he didn't, the relief bursting to life in my chest was stronger than I'd anticipated, making me huff a soundless laugh. He narrowed his eyes at me and started to frown. "Gods damn it, I'm making this worse. I swear I usually have *some* game."

"I'm starting to think your game is Sorry rather than chess." He smiled at his own joke. "I, um...I admit I was disappointed."

I nodded, curling my fingers loosely in the fabric of his shirt. "I'm sorry I didn't do more to help your cause at the meetings."

"Hey." His hands curled around mine and pulled them until he could kiss my fingers, the backs of my hands, turning them to press kisses to the thin skin inside my wrist. "I'm not going to worry about that anymore. We go forward, yeah? I help you find this bell; you help me talk to the council."

"And in the meantime, we go at one another like lustful rabbits?"

"Solid plan, yes." He scooted forward and wrapped his legs around the backs of my thighs, holding me tight with arms and legs as he pulled me in for a kiss. Standing, we had a generous height difference, but with him on the counter, we were close enough in height for our cocks to rub together, the friction of thick denim and wool both making the sensation not enough and too much at the same time. He grunted against my lips, tightening his legs around mine in an effort to get us even closer. "Damn it," he mumbled. "Stupid pants. Who invented these things? I should hex them into next week."

"I think they're super dead by now," I murmured against his neck. He gasped when I slid my hands under his ass, squeezing as I lifted him. "Couch or bed?"

"They're less than four feet apart, so pick one. It's an efficiency."

I staggered us over to the bed, deciding I wanted to spread out. We shucked our clothes with no finesse, alternately grabbing at one another's garments and yanking at our own until we were both bare.

Rowan made an abortive move to cover his soft stomach before sighing and stretching, arms reaching overhead to press against the wall behind the bed. "Hell, you've seen what I look like," he sighed. "It's not like it's a surprise."

"It's nothing short of a delight." I kissed him swiftly before the protest forming on his lips could be given sound. Rowan sighed into the kiss, his tongue dipping past the seam of my lips until I parted for him. He was warmer than Witches I'd been with, far warmer than humans, and I wondered if the smell of his skin, the taste of his mouth, was a Demonborn thing or if Rowan was simply made to press every single one of my pleasure buttons.

I reached to tangle my fingers in his hair only to have him stop me, folding his fingers through mine and tugging until both of us were grasping the headboard. He slid his other hand down my back, short nails scratching at the dip of my spine and drawing a shivering gasp from me. "Fuck! Oh, gods, yes!" Part of me wondered if I should feel at least a little embarrassed about how eager I was, how pliable and needy, but the rest of me told that part to shut the hell up because we were getting laid, and this was *Rowan*, the one I'd been wanking over for months now.

Rowan chuckled breathily before he arched against me, the thick length of his cock sliding against mine, leaving a slick trail of precum I had to break our kiss to taste. I ducked my head, his lips brushing messily against my cheek as I reached down to swipe my finger through the sticky trail on my skin. He made a sound somewhere between a keen and a gasp, shifting so he was lying on his side next to me, not protesting a whit when I pushed him onto his back and slid further down his body, leaving sloppy-sharp bites and licks from his collarbone to his navel.

"Oh!" His gasp was high and sweet when I touched my tongue to the head of his cock, teasing his foreskin with my lips and lapping at his dripping slit. Unable to wait, I wrapped my hand around my own aching erection. I felt the moment when he let go, a static shock of magic rushing over my skin. Mine chased it like a living thing, his sharp and spiky magic finally twisting together with the slow slide of mine. Doors between us opened, his power pouring into mine and mine into his until everything was one blur of color and sensation.

Rowan writhed beneath me, head thrown back to expose that delicate sweep of throat I wanted to bite and mark. His nails scoring my back, I finally gave in to temptation, surging up to leave a small mark just below his Adam's apple. "Fuck, I'm close, and we haven't... Do you... Oh!"

He arched his hips again, his hands sliding down to my ass and grabbing hard. I wanted him to leave marks I could feel for days. I hadn't realized I'd spoken those words aloud until he laughed brokenly. "Okay," he panted, squeezing even harder. I groaned against his collarbone, hips still rocking against his, as he slipped one hand lower, dipping a finger into my crease to tease my hole. He didn't breach it, but the pressure was a delicious tease, making it my turn to writhe against him.

"I won't last much longer," I groaned. "Fuck!"

"There's next time," he promised, pressing against the puckered skin of my opening a tiny bit harder, rolling his hips at the same time. The slide of our hard cocks, slick with precum and spit, our magic sparking everywhere we touched, sent me over the edge. My release started slow, a tightening in my balls racing up my spine and bowing my back. I shouted something (I prayed it wasn't embarrassing) as my cum splashed on his belly. He gasped, high and needy, thrusting faster as my cum slicked the press between our bodies. His own orgasm hit a few moments later, his face beautiful in the contortion of ecstasy.

The warm tickle and tingle of our joined magic ebbed but didn't go entirely away as we lay in his bed, beneath the window with no curtains. The rare snowfall still grayed the sky, the grungy snow globe on the windowsill mirroring the slow swirl of flakes outside. We drifted in and out of sleep. I dreamed only a little, mostly of bells and an angry Egon demanding...something I couldn't decipher.

I finally woke to find the apartment dark save for the orange glow of the streetlights shining through the windows, casting odd shadows between islands of furniture. Rowan was awake and perched on the edge of the bed, tilting his head curiously at the window. "Lay back down," I murmured. "I have to call home tomorrow, talk to Egon, and I want to be rested for that."

He laughed unsteadily but scooted back into my arms. "Sorry. I was just wondering if Chloe had been up here or something."

The thought of his cousin seeing us sprawled, naked and sticky, on his bed was enough to snap me awake. "Christ, you don't think she was, do you?"

"I... I don't know why she would have been. But that snow globe was in my office this morning, and now it's here."

THERE WAS NO USE GOING back to sleep. It was only a bit after ten anyway, well before either of us was used to going to bed. Rowan grabbed the snow globe and took it to the kitchenette, flipping on every light in the apartment as he went. A quick call to Chloe, who was *not* used to being up after ten, told him she had not been upstairs all day, and once the store was closed for the evening, she'd gone straight home. Her roommate could verify. "I tend to believe her. Chloe doesn't lie to me, and her roommate hates her, so for her to offer Chrissy up for an alibi, it must be legit. Chrissy wouldn't help Chloe cover her tracks for love nor money."

"You probably just brought it up with you on accident," I suggested. "When we brought up the box of bells, maybe you grabbed it, too."

"No, it was in my office, not at the front counter. I haven't been in my office since this morning." He was wearing my undershirt and his own briefs, making it very difficult for me to pay attention to anything he was saying. He snapped his fingers in my face. "Hey, eyes up here, buddy."

"Sorry."

"No, you're not." He smiled a little, though, tempering the words.

The smile faded quickly, and he gave the globe a gentle shake, sending the flakes inside flying once more. Inside, a small star rested in the midst of the snow, yellow-painted and once glittery from the looks of things. A few stray pieces of iridescent sparkle still stuck to the paint. The snow itself was dingy, old and cheap. It didn't fit in with the aesthetic of Rowan's space at all.

"Was this a souvenir or something?" I asked. "It looks like something you get at one of those KOA Kamp Trading Posts or something."

"Not so much a souvenir as a posthumous gift. My grandmother loved snow globes. She started collecting them when she was a kid, and it went from picking one up whenever she went on a trip to scouring resale shops for weird ones or ones they didn't make anymore. Had a massive collection of them that got divided up between her kids – my dad and my uncles. This," he shook it again, smiling sadly down at it, "showed up a month or so ago. She'd ordered it online or something, I guess. I mean, she died two years ago, and it only recently arrived? Hell of a back order for this piece of junk."

He gave it a rueful shake. "There was a note with it, one of those things you fill in online, and they print out and shove in the box. It said, 'Rowan, I hope you use this well.' And it was just so weird," he admitted on a wet, shaky laugh. "This thing is kind of ugly, and I'd never even expressed an interest in collecting snow globes, but apparently, she'd decided for me."

I took it from him and shook it hard for a few seconds, making the star disappear behind a minute blizzard. For a moment, I thought I heard the silvery peal of a bell, but it was faint, too soft to truly make out. "She probably just thought she'd like to have a common interest with you."

"Maybe," Rowan muttered but didn't sound convinced. "Well. I guess we should discuss logistics about this council thing."

We set the snow globe on the coffee table beside the box of bells. While Rowan made us cups of mint tea and a plate of snacks, I sent a message to Egon, telling him that I'd found twelve of the thirteen bells but would be getting the last one soon, and I needed to request a formal meeting of the Witch council before Solstice. Egon had not responded, but I wasn't terribly surprised. He'd be asleep back home by now. If he even slept. Come to think of it, I didn't think I'd ever seen the man so much as yawn.

"We meet at Solstice because the veil is thinnest, and it was also the first time we were led to the Wellspring." Rowan cut me a glance, but he didn't argue. I pressed on. "The Winter Solstice meeting for the Witches has become the time when, traditionally, we cut our losses, get rid of things we don't want to take into the new year with us, and also start any new projects. Or at least name them and claim them."

He picked up the snow globe again and gave it a gentle shake. The snow flurried around the tiny star. Cradling the globe in his hands, he hummed thoughtfully. "And the Revelation is the project this year," he said, not a question.

"Mmm. Well, it's not just Witches. The entire Grand Council wants it voted on next week." They'd wanted it voted on for a century's worth of *next weeks,* but it was finally, finally happening. That knowledge was both exasperating and terrifying.

"Without Demonborn giving any input," he sighed, sounding resigned. "Reveal to humans that yes, Witches and Faeries and, hell, even mermaids and Bigfoot are real, but leave Demons out of it." He reached out to put the snow globe back down on the coffee table but missed, hitting the edge. The plastic globe tumbled out of his grasp. Before he could fumble, it hit the floor and broke open, spilling a small puddle of old water, grubby plastic bits, and one poorly painted gold star. "Oh, shit. God damn it." He surged to his feet, heading for the kitchen to grab paper towels.

"Rowan..."

He brushed me aside, dropping down to mop up the water and scoop the plastic bits into a small pile. "I hated that thing," he admitted gruffly. "But it was from her somehow, you know? Back order, or maybe Chloe thinking she was doing a nice thing by pretending...I don't know. But it was Heliotrope's, and now..." He picked up the tiny star and winced as a broken corner drew a bead of blood from his palm. "Oh, I give up," he muttered, dropping to sit on his heels.

"Let me." Nudging him gently aside, I wiped up the rest of the water and fake snow, sweeping the broken pieces of plastic into the dustpan he'd brought over with the paper towels. Dumping it in the trash, I rescued the plastic star and carried it back over to him. He rolled his eyes halfheartedly but took it, tucking it into his palm and smearing it with blood.

"I'm sorry," I offered. "Come here." He let me pull him into a hug there on the floor, tangling our legs uncomfortably, but neither of us wanted to move. "Huh. It's snowing harder again."

"Good Lord. I must've hit a vein or something when I made it snow this morning. This," he waved one tired finger at the window, "hasn't been me in hours."

"Sometimes weather is just weather," I noted. "Not everything comes down to magic."

He snorted. "Yeah, I know."

We were quiet for a long time before, finally, he spoke again. "So, here's what I'm thinking. We drive up north. Have this meeting, give back the bells because, hello, goodwill gesture, right? I mean, no way in Hell was I going to keep them or anything, but it's all about the optics."

"You sound like a born politician."

"Hush your mouth," he chastised. "Now. Have the meeting. Then, if things go well, yay, Solstice time. If they don't, then...well, then, I'll get a flight back here, and that's it for a year and a day."

He was sitting stiffly in my lap, perched on one of my knees, not quite meeting my gaze.

"If they turn down your request, then we'll work on something for next time," I insisted. "Rowan, I'm not throwing you to the wolves here."

"No, just a bunch of Witches."

WE PLANNED THE ROAD trip to leave in two days' time, giving us enough of a window to pack. Not that I had a lot to do—I never had made it to the hotel, and all my things were still in my rental car parked on the street. We also agreed to do some road-trip-snack grocery shopping. Meanwhile, Rowan made arrangements with Chloe to keep an eye on the shop and asked his brother Ellery to keep an eye on things just in case. Chloe seemed fully capable, but I had a feeling she was the baby in the family, and no one would let her forget it. "I'm sad you're not going to be here for Solstice," she said when she came out to hug him goodbye. "I'm making a log and everything!"

"Last time you did the log, you packed it with firecrackers left over from the Fourth and damn near gave Uncle Al a heart attack." They shared a grin. "Take video this year."

"Uncle Al?" I slung my bag into the trunk of the car. "I thought everyone in your family had plant names or names to do with springtime and the like."

"Al is short for Algaric," Chloe said with a totally straight face. "Like the poison mushroom."

"Seriously?"

Rowan snickered. "Come on. I'll get us out of Houston, and then it's your turn to drive."

"No, but, seriously...Algaric?"

As Chloe waved from the sidewalk, Rowan crept out into the still-snowy street and pointed us towards the freeway. "All right," he said. "Your job is to keep me awake. Tell me everything I need to know to survive this."

CHAPTER FIVE

O*f course, there was only one room left at the inn*

ROWAN

The first day, the drive north was beautiful but exceedingly boring. "Fucking Hell, we should've just flown the whole way."

"I suggested it," Whitaker reminded me as we left a Bucc-ee's somewhere in Texarkana. "But you wanted to do it this way."

I'd wanted to spend more time with him and had been afraid flying up would end things too soon. And neither of us trusted the bells in checked baggage. We'd reach the Frost compound, where the meeting was to be held, by the twentieth, one day before the Solstice. Whitaker assured me plenty of other people would be around, not involved with the meeting or ritual, just other Witches and beings who wanted to be with others like themselves at the holidays.

"You'll have met most of them, from all the meetings." I must have made a face, or maybe his Witchy vibes picked up something because he patted my leg, glancing away from the road before returning his attention to the thickening traffic. Giving my thigh a squeeze, he added, "Think of it as a networking opportunity, if that helps."

It didn't.

He'd also been in touch with Egon, who seemed to find a reason to call every hour or so. Whenever Whitaker had him on speaker, Egon had sounded pleased on the surface, but the underlying edge to his words made me uncomfortable. I found myself fiddling with the little plastic star from the snow globe every time Egon's name popped up on caller ID, which it did more frequently as our first day on the road headed towards evening. The calls went from 'just checking to make sure the trip is going well' to more aggressive and detailed discussions of Witch clan politics and Solstice ritual planning. They left Whitaker with a headache and me feeling awkward every time. One of the few times Egon deigned to speak with me directly, he informed me he'd known my grandmother for several years before she passed and called her tenacious. When he said the word, it sounded less complimentary and more insulting.

"She was definitely that," I agreed, earning a sharp look from Whitaker.

"I was a bit surprised she'd known Madam Frost," Egon continued. We were rocketing towards Memphis and our hotel for the night, and I just wanted this asshat to shut up so I could try and enjoy the rest of the evening. "I had to ask a few of our elder members, but they remember Lucinda and Heliotrope being quite close for many years when they were younger until reason prevailed, and they drifted."

Hackles were officially up.

He then demanded I hand the phone to Whitaker, and no, he didn't care the boy was driving, and absolutely not, he would not be put on speakerphone.

I let Whitaker take over the conversation, informing Egon we'd be there by the twentieth and everything else could wait. He didn't try to get me to talk about the conversation at all. Until we reached the hotel for the night, we were both stiff and quiet. Whitaker took care of check-in while I pretended to give a damn about the array of colorful brochures advertising tourist attractions and scammy deals on tours around the city. Eschewing the elevator creaking with some sort of electrical asthma and a ghost lurking by the keypad, we lugged our bags up to the second floor, tossing our things gracelessly onto the beds.

"I didn't want to assume," Whitaker said, gesturing towards the lumpy double beds arranged a foot or so apart.

I nodded. "Thanks." We both stared around the room like we'd never been in a mid-range motel before. Like we hadn't been all over each other forty-eight hours ago.

Awkward. As. Balls.

"Do you want to shower?" Whitaker's eyes went wide, and the man had the audacity to blush as he fumbled, "I mean, do you want to go first? Otherwise, I'm gonna just go...um. Gonna go try to drown myself." He spun on his heel and hurried the few steps to the small, plastic bathroom, shutting the door with a click.

A moment later, there was a dull thud like he'd bopped his head against it. After a pause, the shower creaked to life. I found his bag, setting it outside the bathroom door. Eventually, he'd realize he'd tore into there without a change of clothes, and, as nice as it would have been to see him saunter out in his altogether, it probably would've made things even more uncomfortable.

I opted for the bed closer to the industrial-strength air conditioner, scrunching up the weird foam comforter and shoving it into one corner of the room before kicking off my shoes, climbing onto the exceedingly firm mattress, and dragging my phone out of my hip pocket. Three messages from Chloe awaited me.

Chloe: Hey. So just as an FYI, two Witches came by today but weren't like regular customers for the woo woo stuff.

Chloe: And a Faerie. I think a Sidhe. Really tall, super pretty, and scary. Sniffed at me.

Chloe: Dude, I'm sleeping in your apartment tonight. Chrissy is such a bitch! Call me.

The shower was still raging, so I gave in and called my cousin. Chloe answered on the third ring. "Oh, my fucking God," she said by way of greeting. "I think those stupid bells cursed me or something!"

"Hey, Chloe. Yeah, the drive was really boring, but we made it to the hotel all right. If I ever see another Big Gulp, I might puke, but you know how it goes."

"Wow that was...so suburban dad."

"That's just cruel!"

She blew a raspberry down the line, the crackle of sound jarring and painful. While I yelped and cursed, she laughed and apologized, both of us winding down into a mutual sigh of *meh*.

"So," she said after a moment, "do you want me to start with the Witches, the Faerie, or the bitch?"

"Oh, let's work backward. What'd Chrissy do?"

"She drank my tea."

"Um. I like tea as much as the next caffeine addict, but that's hardly worth sleeping at my place over."

"She drank it in bed. With that guy I've been seeing."

"Oh. Well. Yeah, then. That's...yikes."

"And it wouldn't have been so bad if I hadn't just been sniffed by a freaking Faerie," she added, her tone ratcheting up a notch. "Seriously! They were all pretty and glowy and acting like their shit wouldn't stink. They *sniffed* me, Ro. Not even a sneaky sniff, like they thought I was hot and wanted to see if I smelled good. Just a full-on *do I smell something spoiled* snootful!"

"We get Fae folk in the store sometimes." I sat up on the creaky bed. The shower was still running, and I was half-tempted to throw open the door and demand to know how many layers of skin he felt the need to scrub off after sitting beside me for ten hours. I was considering going in there with a polite knock and putting Chloe on speaker because I had a hinky feeling in my gut about her day and thought maybe, if he wasn't in there taking a thorough scrub-down, another set of ears might be helpful.

"Dude, did you not hear me about the sniffing? I swear they were like marking me or something."

"If they were marking you, we'd be having a very different conversation. Look," I sighed, flopping back against the thin pillows, "Ellery and his new human-lite boyfriend are stirring up a lot of interest in some quarters. No matter how chill and lowkey they try to be, magicals are talking."

And I kind of hated being enough in the gossip loop to know about the issue, but at the same time, it was coming in fairly useful lately whenever I'd catch wind of someone with negative shit to say about my brother. Usually, they labored under the misapprehension I would agree with them, that he was somehow bringing shame to Demonborn, and that his new little friend (who wasn't really new—hello, college roommate) would destroy the whole Revelation thing. They got charged the *you're being an asshole about my family* fee on top of sales tax. And if they started trying to get me to pass messages to Ellery and Simon or feel me out for inside intel on how the whole worst-kept secret of a human liaison in potentia was going to work, I added a *get the hell out of my store* surcharge.

Chloe huffed an annoyed corgi sound. "Look, all I'm saying is it was weird. He was up to something."

"I'm not doubting you." I did absolutely believe she felt that way, but I was having a difficult time discerning why a Sidhe would be smelling around at all. "If they come back, call me immediately. I'll have my phone on and with me for the rest of the trip."

"Oh? Even at night?"

"It's night now, so..."

"I would hate to interrupt anything."

I could hear her smirk. "Good night, Chloe."

"Wait! Wait, wait, wait!"

"Swear to gods, if this is so you can wink wink nudge nudge at me..." The shower shut off, and a funny little trill of excitement raced down my chest and settled in my belly. The irrational desire for Whitaker to wander out naked and damp, his chest and throat pink from the heat of the shower as he looked up and remembered he wasn't alone...

I might have had a very active imagination. Very active and very vivid.

"It's not," Chloe sighed. "It's something I remembered I forgot earlier but should've remembered to tell you before you left, so you could take it into account, but I just now remembered I forgot so—"

"Breathe."

"Ugh. Okay, so how far are y'all from Pine Bluff?"

As I groaned, Whitaker opened the door. He paused, one hand still on the knob (doorknob, thank you very much) and the other clutching a white hotel towel around his hips. He widened his eyes at the sight of me sprawled on the bed. *Okay*? he mouthed.

I shook my head. "Chloe," I sighed, and he nodded, rolling his eyes as he carefully bent to grab his bag and backed into the bathroom again. Damn it. "We're outside of Little Rock. Why do I need to go to Pine Bluff?"

"I never said you needed to go to Pine Bluff."

"Seriously?"

"Ugh, okay. Regina Greenbaum has a massive armoire she wanted appraised and said she'll only trust you to do it."

"Regina Greenbaum lives in Rice Village." I named the wealthy, ancient neighborhood in Houston full of older mini-mansions and money aged enough to have grand-money in exclusive Montessori schools across town. Regina Greenbaum had been a client and friend of my grandmother's for decades, a formidable old Demon rumored to have a greenhouse full of plants she'd enchanted to be especially vicious. That was a pernicious rumor, though; the greenhouse was full of orchids, and they were perfectly ordinary, if a bit snooty. "Why would she have an armoire in Arkansas?"

"She bought it at an estate sale. Or her grandson bought it for her. I'm not sure. But it's at some old house in Pine Bluff, and she wants it appraised before she has it moved so she can get insurance on it."

"She is aware other people could take care of it for her? People who already live in Arkansas?"

I could practically hear Chloe's shrug. "She said it had to be you. She suggested you just sigil-travel yourself there and back so she could have an answer before tomorrow night."

"Did you tell her I was out of town?"

Whitaker reappeared, wearing a black t-shirt worn thin with age and a pair of sweatpants doing the Lord's work. The thin strip of skin across his back I could see when he bent to shove his bag under the bed distracted me so much I missed what Chloe said.

"Wait, come again?"

She snorted but admirably didn't turn it into a sex joke. At least not out loud. "I didn't tell her you were out, no. She seemed to think something was weird, though, since you weren't in the shop. She kept asking if you were okay since she'd never been here when you weren't, not since Grandma died." I could hear her turn the TV on in my den and the Netflix start-up sound. She was done with the call, even if I wasn't. "She said she'd check back tomorrow. Hey, why didn't you two just sigil-travel up there?"

"You know why," I muttered.

It was my great failing as a Demonborn. Sigil-travel terrified me. I was only passably decent at it, and the greater the distance, the worse my anxiety became. Once, I'd managed to get myself stuck Between for what felt like days but was only an hour before my father pulled me out by my hair and scolded me for embarrassing him in front of the clan and Watchers.

"You just want to spend more time with your Witchy-poo," she singsonged.

"Hey!" I mean, she wasn't wrong, but still...

"Look, I'll text you the address, okay? Hop over there, take a look, do your thing, and send me the info so I can give it to her. Love you. Mwah."

"It's not that easy. There's official paperwork I need to fill out and—" She was already gone. I flopped my arms out to either side and groaned loud and long. "Fuck," I said on the tail end of the guttural sound.

"Good talk?" Whitaker asked, turning the TV on and flipping through the channels far too quickly for someone intending to find a show to watch. He was nervous, I thought, and fidgeting, trying to look like he was doing something other than waiting to see what *I'd* do.

"Maybe. Kind of? Do you mind if we take a little side trip tomorrow?"

He groaned. Even though I knew it was a sound of frustration, it zapped straight to my balls and did *things* to me. *Things*.

"We're on a schedule, Rowan. The Solstice—"

"Is still on the twenty-first. Pine Bluff is not that far." I hoped. I wasn't really sure; I'd look it up when he wasn't paying attention. "I need to appraise something for a longtime client."

"Who just happened to know you were in Arkansas?" he asked, one brow winging upward. "I thought you weren't going to spread the info around."

"I didn't. She asked Chloe if it could be arranged." I fiddled with my phone then, a mirror of his earlier fidgeting. "It's not unusual for one of Grandma's long-term clients to ask for something to be appraised out of town." Of course, that was usually somewhere like Austin or Galveston. Usually, items out of state were appraised by the seller first. "Hm."

"Yeah, just noticing how weird it sounds?"

I tossed one of my pillows at him, regretting it when he shoved it behind his back, clearly intent on staking his claim.

"Mrs. Greenbaum is a nice-ish old lady. If she had some nefarious plot against me, I'd have known already. She's nice but not subtle."

"Nice-ish."

"Well. She's very brusque."

Whitaker was quiet for several long minutes, during which Chloe texted me the address for Mrs. Greenbaum's armoire. Finally, he sighed. "There's a weird vibration around this."

But he muttered it, so it sounded, at first, like *deer wear libations in skins,* which was weird, even for a Witch. "Do what now?"

Whitaker rolled onto one hip, not quite meeting my eyes while he looked sternly awkward. "There's a weird vibration around this." He wiggled the fingers of his left hand in the air. "I can feel it. The magic equivalent of something being out of tune."

Shit. "I think if Regina Greenbaum was trying to do something," I wiggled my fingers in the air in imitation of his gesture, "Chloe would've picked up on it. I know she seems kind of ding-batty, but she's sharp as a tack, and she *is* really a Demonborn. We're pretty familiar with..." I wiggled my fingers again.

Whitaker shook his head. "I don't doubt you are, but something's just very off about this. Fuck. Okay, this is...this is awkward. Do you mind if I check something?"

"Er, go for it." I scooched further up the bed, folding and squishing my remaining pancake of a pillow around to try and get comfortable. I didn't notice, at first, what Whitaker was doing. When I finally glanced up, it was like running into your kindergarten teacher at a bar. You know they're an adult but seeing them actually adulting is disorienting. Seeing Whitaker doing something Witchy was definitely unbalancing.

Settled on the floor, a slim, wide wooden box open in front of him, he arranged several stones and a small jar of what I hoped was salt in a pattern atop a star with way more points than I was used to seeing burned into the wood of the lid. Glancing up at me, he smiled tightly. "One point for each of the original twelve clans and—"

"And one for the stranger," I said, nodding. "Okay. And this is checking something?"

"In as much as I can, with limited resources." He made a shooing motion at me and closed his eyes. I settled back and, for a long moment, tried to look at anything other than him. Gaping as he engaged in some Witch ritual felt weird, but soon a warm, soft, fizzy feeling crept over me. Rather than energizing, it was calming. "It's okay to stare," he murmured, eyes still closed. "I trust you."

That fizzed harder than the magic. *Why,* I almost asked. The word was on the edge of my teeth before I clamped down hard and swallowed it back. He had no reason to, certainly not simply because we'd had mutual orgasms and we found each other aesthetically pleasing. I mean, I liked to think maybe he liked me as more than a curiosity—the one Demonborn he could stand. Or, in my grimmer turns of thought, the trophy Demonborn he'd fucked around with and could boast of to the other Witches, proof of the way he could make a Demon beg. Make a Demon vulnerable.

Whitaker frowned, inhaling sharply through his nose and reaching for the jar. "Whatever you're thinking so hard about, stop for the next few minutes, please. You're throwing me off." He uncapped the jar and tipped a few teaspoonfuls of the granules into the center of the wood-burned design.

My first reaction, which was admittedly to flounce off in embarrassment, was quelled by a voice that sounded quite a bit like Madame Frost's in the back of my thoughts. *Sit down, shut up, and learn something.*

Learn what, though? I would never do Witch magic, just like he'd never do Demon magic.

If you want to be part of this whole flea circus, you need to untangle the vine.

Even as the voice of my subconscious, Madame Frost was slightly confusing and prone to butchering metaphor.

The warm-fizz calm tickled along my arms and throat once more, whatever Whitaker was doing picking up in intensity. He moved a few of the stones along the lines of the star, scattering the salt he'd spilled in the center circle. Hands resting on his knees, Whitaker sat straighter, his lips moving over words I couldn't make out as he breathed them over the tools in front of him. After a few long moments, the stones shone with a faint gleam, not so much a glow as an aura. Like they'd pushed through to some other layer of the world, shining with sunlight from that other place. The salt hissed along the lines of the star, settling in two of the shallow troughs.

Whitaker held his right hand palm down over the entire thing and quietly murmured something in a language, curly and sharp at the same time. He closed his fingers quickly like he was grabbing something out of the air. Immediately, the aura snapped out, and the fizz along my skin stopped. Whitaker didn't open his eyes for several breaths. Finally, he glanced at me, offered a shy, almost awkward smile, and brought his hand up to his face, slowly opening his fingers like he was afraid whatever was behind them might escape.

A tiny glimmer of green, pale as a new spring leaf, shone for a fraction of a blink. It was gone so fast I thought I was overtired, and my eyes were acting up.

Sighing, Whitaker folded in on himself somehow. He didn't slump or fall over so much as just...became less-than. I hadn't realized how far out he'd pushed his power, thinking he'd been entirely focused on the board and whatever he'd been doing there. But he'd shoved it out past me, maybe even past the walls of the room itself. "Are you okay?" I asked quietly.

He nodded. "It's not my preferred method of intel gathering, but it does the trick in a pinch." He passed a hand over his face, scrubbing at tired eyes before turning his attention to his set-up, packing it all away efficiently. He tipped the salt into his hand and looked around for a moment before his gaze settled on me. "I know it's unorthodox, but got a light?"

"I don't smoke. Oh, wait, I get it..." I slid from the bed and ended up on my knees across from him.

"It's not...tainted." He made a face at the word choice. "There's no magic left in it." He shook his closed fist slightly and nodded at me.

"Oh, right." I let him tip it into my hand, carefully brushing each grain into my own palm. Burning the salt away didn't take much effort, letting the hidden flame of my own magic rise to the surface, pulling from the eternally deep well all Demonborn could access. After a minute, all that was left was a smear of a yellowish residue on my skin that rubbed off on my jeans.

Whitaker gazed at me intensely, his expression unreadable as he stared at my mouth. *He wants to kiss me.* I licked my lips, hoping it came off as seductive rather than dehydrated. It seemed to drag his attention back, though, whichever way it looked, because he blinked, shook his head, and smiled at me.

"I was right about it being weird. My fetch says Witch magic is being stirred against Demonborn along this line here." He tapped one of the lines in the star.

I guessed kissing was off the table. Which, to be fair, was probably the best course of action for the time being. Damn it.

"I'm sorry, your what now?"

"Fetch." He paused in his packing of the box. "Surely even a Demon has heard of a fetch."

"I can't tell if you're yanking my chain or not."

His sly smile told me he probably was.

"I thought you were the Demonborn's expert on the history of Witches and magic."

"Huh? Where'd you get that idea?" He pushed himself to his feet, and I followed, standing back as he set the still-open box on the bed he'd chosen. He'd tucked the stones back into a small leather pouch, and the salt jar was sealed tight. The fizz of magic was gone, but I knew better than to touch. I remembered what happened with the bells.

Whitaker shrugged, his smirk curling into something not quite a smile but definitely amused. "Granmere said quite a few times that your knowledge of our history was unusual for one of your lot."

One of my lot? That stung more than a little. "Well, know thy enemy and all that."

"I thought we weren't enemies." He settled on the bed with the box between us and gestured for me to sit. Gingerly, I perched on the corner, not quite willing to settle back. I wasn't necessarily afraid of the magic, but I was cautious, and he noticed. "It's not charmed. Or hexed. Or whatever you're worried about. It's merely a tool I use for channeling my fetch."

"There's that word again."

He held out the bag of stones. "These are from my home. My family's home. It's...it's a strange place," he chuckled. "Have you ever been? I don't mean my grandmother's house. The one my parents live in now. The one I grew up in." He shook the bag, making the stones rattle. "Mother's hosted a few of the smaller meetings there."

"I've never been. It's rather hard to find." Bespelled to be so, which wasn't exactly a secret. The Frosts were older than dirt, powerful, and eccentric. Even for Witches.

Whitaker's smile was fond, a little sheepish. "My family has a very hard time letting go of things." He gently shook the stones. "These are from different parts of the house. One is from the original hovel, so old none of us can remember the name of the ancestor who lived there. One is from a castle, where Lydia's bedroom is right now. One is from—"

"Wait, wait, wait. Her bedroom is a castle?" I wondered if I could suddenly develop telekinesis and get one of the tiny, overpriced bottles of booze from the minibar to head my way without having to give up my comfortable perch on the bed. "Run that by me again."

CHAPTER SIX

It's the most wtf time of the year.

WHITAKER

I've had friends, usually humans, who felt awkward about their homes. When I was a boy and would go to a friend's place, a parent always gave a flutter of apologies (or, honestly, a staff member; Mother liked to make sure we were friends with the 'right' crowd) about how much of a mess the place was, or some other ridiculous thing kids gave zero shits about. And when I got older, my friends muttered about the clutter, the lack of space, whatever it was I was meant to find offensive about where they lived but honestly never did. Why would I give two damns if someone had last year's drapes or their media room had a sixty-inch screen instead of a plasma whatever? Or if they even had a media room?

Until an embarrassingly late point in my early adulthood, it didn't occur to me they were comparing their homes to my family's. That the chaos and mismatched bits and weird doors to nowhere overlaid with sleek lines and modern fittings were enviable to others, at least those in our circles. Other Witch clans had old homes, ancestral palaces even. Those who didn't still kept some connection to their roots, whether through some bit of magic or some personal artifacts—stones moved from across the ocean and laid in the garden maybe, or wood from sacred trees felled by humans, taken and turned into tables, floors, altars. Every Witch found a way to surround ourselves with our ancestor's magic, even if only a small bag of stones plucked from around the house where they grew up.

"Our house is...unusual," I finally said. Rowan's brows twitched slightly upwards. "I mean, even by Witch standards. We're one of the oldest clans, and our magic is...it's strong." I barely kept myself from admitting to Rowan one of our deep family secrets: There was a very good chance the Frosts no longer needed the Wellspring, that our line of magic was old and uninterrupted enough to carry on without the renewal. None of us had been bold enough to test it yet and know for certain.

Rowan leaned back on his hands, leveling a bored expression at me. "This is precious and all, but unless you have a point to make, I'm losing interest fast and would like a shower before hitting the rack, especially if we're detouring to Pine Bluff." He raised a brow at me, a silent challenge in his expression.

He wanted to argue, I thought, or at least change the subject to something that could lead to an argument. Rowan didn't like to pick fights, not really. At least as far as I knew. But he never backed down from a fair one or one he thought was unfairly biased against a weaker opponent. It crossed my mind that he didn't like arguments, but he felt safe with them. He knew where he stood, didn't have to try and tread carefully. When he argued, he threw his entire self into it.

I'd seen him go 'round with Council members more than once, arguing for his presence to be recorded in the minutes, demanding they retract something specious with regards to Demons or, more lately, humans (in no small part thanks to his brother taking up with a former Changeling, I was certain). Sitting at the foot of my bed now, Rowan was uncertain and uneasy. Getting into an argument with me would put him on familiar ground.

I hated to burst his bubble, but...

"The family home is composed of bits and pieces of places the family has lived over the years. It's held together largely by complicated magic—"

"Isn't everything?" he muttered.

Touché. "Generations of spell-work, carefully mapped out and interwoven," I continued, trying not to smile a little at his snark. "When a predecessor passes, part of their home is woven into the whole."

"And the part where Lydia's room is..."

"Was, and is, part of a castle, yes." It was really nice, truth be told. Not damp and drafty at all. But that was largely thanks to the room having been woven into the house by a recently departed relative, after the invention of indoor plumbing and electric lights, Lydia having a very strong talent for interior design, and an Amex black card.

Rowan shifted to lean forward, his bored expression gone, replaced by wide-eyed amusement. "What was your room?"

"My room is in a rather nice apartment in midtown Manhattan," I said tartly. "I don't live with my parents."

"But you used to." He shifted again, bringing one leg up onto the bed, close enough for our knees to touch. "Another castle? Some fancy French chateau? All gilt and white with fancy-ass statuary?"

I smirked, feeling a shadow of a blush heat my cheeks, and shrugged. "Just a regular bedroom. It had been part of a Frost family home in Charleston, so it's nothing very fancy at all."

Okay, I was underselling it. It was woven in from a mansion and had its own fireplace and hardwood floors. Plus, it featured a skylight that shouldn't exist at all but always showed a beautiful, unchanging view of the night sky since it was what Charmaine Frost, my third cousin once removed or something, had been looking at as she passed and breathed the spell into completion.

Morbid, but soothing, really.

Lips quirking into a thoughtful twist, he regarded me in silence for a very long moment. "Okay, then. And what does any of that have to do with your board game here?"

I shook the bag again. "Each stone is from a different part of the house. They're imbued with my family's magic, powerful Witch magic going back centuries made even stronger by the fact the stones are part of a still-living spell. The salt is sea salt, but it makes no difference really—"

"I'm aware," he said, though it lacked the bite I had expected from him. He could be very defensive when it came to his knowledge of magical accouterments "Salt is salt is salt, no matter what Gwyneth Paltrow says."

That time, I did snort. "Right. Well, I use the stones to draw on energy without depleting my own too badly, and the salt is for...well. You know."

"Purification, blocking, and fries."

"Good boy." He made a small sound, more annoyed than pleased, but the idea had taken root in my thoughts, and I made a note to revisit it later for research purposes. "A fetch is part of a Witch's essence."

"Ew."

"Spirit, then, you child. Part of our fundamental energy. Fetches are old magic and can cause harm to the sender if something happens to it."

"So, if someone stabs your fetch..."

"That's oddly specific," I said slowly, "but yes, that would affect me directly. More so if it was a magical attack. A bespelled blade, for example."

Rowan nodded thoughtfully. "So, you set up your magical backgammon board, drew on your ancestral energy, threw down some salt just in case, and..." He looked at the plain star burned into the wood. "Okay, I'm at a loss. What did this do?"

"Protection," I said shrugging. "It can be any shape at all, really, but a star is traditional. When I send out my fetch, this," I tapped the board, "acts as a safe place to land, so to speak. It helps me focus my magic for the working, and it also gives the fetch a spot to return to before I take it back into myself."

I hesitated. While there were few rules on the books when it came to what we could and couldn't share with Demons specifically, treading really freaking lightly was another tradition. And it was a hard one to shake, to be honest. No matter how much I trusted—or wanted to trust—Rowan, I couldn't quite bring myself to say the words. Before I took that piece of magic, of my very spirit, back into myself, it passed through the spells and charms I'd set on the board, charged with the stones and salt, cleansed of any taint from wherever I'd sent it.

"Did you just say *taint*?"

"I...no?" My brain to mouth filter was offline, apparently, and, judging by the heat creeping up my throat to my face, had taken my internal thermostat with it. Super. I'd never felt sexier in my life. Rowan leaned closer, his brows creeping up. "I said 'flaint.' Which is an ancient word in the language of Witches. It means, um...it means..."

"Dude, you were so saying the loud part quiet and the quiet part loud, weren't you?" Rowan's grin was quicksilver. "Tell me about this magical taint."

"Er..."

"Seriously, all you said was something under your breath about cleansing a taint." His brows twitched, and I knew he was trying not to laugh. "Is this foreplay? Because I have to be honest, it's not exactly doing it for me, but I'm okay with seeing how this plays out. I'd say I'd never seen a magical taint, but I guess I can count my own as magical since, you know, Demon and all."

My brain did one of those weird record-scratch noises. "You look at your own taint?"

"Well, yeah." He shrugged. "Who doesn't, at least once? It's important to be familiar with your body, especially if you're into orgasms." He paused, and that quicksilver smile was back. "Or certain piercings. Or both."

"What, um...what kind of piercings would you mean?" I wasn't entirely naive. I knew how to use the internet. I'd seen things. But... "I mean, is that...are you into that?"

Rowan's laugh startled the butterflies in my stomach back into wakefulness. "You're losing the thread." He tapped the bed next to the board. "Look, you don't have to break it all down for me. I don't need to know the details to know it's Witch magic. I just wanted to know what you were doing and why."

"Ah. Well."

"You wanted to know about Pine Bluff," he urged softly. "What did you find out?"

"The fetch discerned powerful Demon magic at work, which is why the salt hissed." I glanced up at him, wondering if he was going to be offended or touchy.

He nodded. "Makes sense. Most Demons would have something in their work to keep snoops out." He rolled his eyes. "Don't look so affronted. You just admitted you were snooping. So." He slapped his hands on his knees and stood. "This is super interesting and all, but if you've satisfied yourself we're not walking into some massive death trap tomorrow, I'm gonna get some sleep. I need my beauty rest."

He didn't head for the bed, though. He grabbed a few things out of his luggage and went into the bathroom. After a moment, the shower hissed to life, and he sighed loudly and deeply with what sounded like pleasure. I busied myself with putting my tools away, a wave of guilt sloshing through me.

Every Witch since as far back as we had records was either staunchly anti-Demon or largely ignored by the community when they tried to change minds. My grandmother was the only Witch I'd ever known who thought being so stingy with our magic toward Demons was ridiculous. We'd give spells to Sidhe, cast a bit of an enchantment for the merpeople when they surfaced from their undersea homes. We'd nudge favorite humans with a bit of luck magic, and hell, we threw it around pretty liberally ourselves. Those of us with jobs outside the community usually had to undergo a very fast, damn near brutal reconditioning about using magic in human spaces. The first time I closed my office door with a wave of my fingers, I nearly gave my secretary a heart attack. Thankfully, she believed it was indeed merely a weird occurrence, and yes, she probably bumped it and didn't notice.

But few of us—very few of us—would simply chat about magic so casually with a Demon. And no matter how I felt about Rowan, no matter how hard he was working to ensure his lot joined with the rest of us on the Council, I felt that slick slide of guilt in my belly and pushing against my chest. I'd shown a Demon something intimate with my magic. I'd let him watch me. I'd explained it to him as best I could. And he'd been interested. Not in a threatening way, but truly interested.

I stretched out on the narrow bed I'd chosen and tried to at least pretend to be settling in for the night. A few minutes later, Rowan exited the bathroom in a waft of pine-scented steam, a minty toothbrush hanging from the corner of his mouth as he hummed. Clutching a towel around his waist, he didn't even glance at me. He crouched by his bag and pulled out a pair of extremely bright blue underpants, a t-shirt, and a pair of dark gray joggers before heading back into the bathroom.

"Hey," he called after spitting into the sink. "Want to watch a movie or something?" He stuck his head back out. "I can't sleep for shit. I can tell already I'll be up all night. Pick something that doesn't suck." He grabbed the remote off the TV stand and chucked it in my direction. I caught it midair with a twist of my fingers, bringing it to me in a slow arc. He grinned, slightly foamy, and winked before disappearing into the bathroom one more time.

By the time he finally emerged, hair in damp curls and skin scrubbed pink, smelling of pine and spice and toothpaste, I'd settled on a big-budget superhero movie. He feigned disgust but settled in on the other bed easily enough. I thought about suggesting we order a pizza, but the air between us felt too fragile, a polished-thin eggshell that would shatter if you looked at it the wrong way.

"You're doing that thing with your eye," he said sometime around the first big skirmish, the one where we're supposed to think our hero is going to be too weak to fight the final boss, that he's lost some of whatever made him awesome in the previous movies.

"Blinking? Seeing?"

"No," he drew out. "That thing where you kind of scrunch up the right one and look like maybe you're seeing something far away but only on one side. You make that face when you're not sure about something."

I turned to look at him. He was staring at Hottie McHunk, watching the hero and his oiled-up torso kneel at the feet of the leather-clad Big Bad.

I'm pretty sure the aesthetics weren't accidental and birthed a thousand kinky fanfics.

"How do you know what I look like when I'm worried?"

"I didn't say you looked worried. I said you looked like you weren't sure about something. When you worry, you make this sour face. Like this." Still looking at the screen, he jutted his lower lip out slightly and pinched it between thumb and forefinger.

I was about to protest, but I'd been doing the same thing while he was showering, and my fingers were reaching up to do it again even as I stared at him. He finally looked at me and quirked his eyebrow in that way that made my stomach do a funny little lurch. Entirely unbecoming a Witch of my age and status.

But *ugh,* that eyebrow thing? So hot.

"I've seen you make the same face pretty often at Council meetings. Usually right before you ask for clarification or order a suggestion tabled until further research can be done. So, tell me." He shifted to lay on his side facing me, one hand tucked under his cheek and the other draped over his waist. "What's got you making the face now? Is it the sheer impossibility of Abs McGee falling from space and not bursting into flames on reentry? Or are you wondering if it's too late to strip the comforter off the bed because you know how gross it is?"

My mouth hung open, words dying on my tongue. "Huh?"

He smirked, then burst into a full-on cackle. "Oh, my gods, you're adorable when you're off balance. Conversationally," he added. "If you were really off balance, I wouldn't be laughing. Unless you were like doing some flaily thing on ice skates or something. Then all bets are off."

"I'll keep that in mind in the morning. It's supposed to snow overnight."

He drummed the fingers of his free hand against his stomach. "I'll let you change the subject this time," he allowed after a long, quiet moment. "But you can't keep dodging questions. My patience is worse than Alastor's, and he's so impatient he was born six weeks early because he had things to do on the outside."

I chuckled weakly. "I haven't met him, but impatience and stubbornness seem to run in the Hebert family. You, Ellery," I ticked off on my fingers, "your grandmother."

He sighed, not a sad sound but one of tiredness and maybe a bit of remembering. "Heliotrope was definitely stubborn. But mostly when it came to things that were right."

"And she always thought her way was right?" I teased gently.

Heliotrope Hebert always exuded a stern sort of certainty, not unkind but just...firm. She and Grandmere had gotten on very well, so well Granmere trusted her with Simon, her pet project of a human who ended up being Ellery Hebert's new boyfriend. Well, newish. They'd been together long enough now I was sure some of the glow had dimmed a bit.

But maybe I was wrong. My longest relationship had been less than a year because he felt I was keeping secrets. He wasn't wrong. I simply couldn't bring myself to tell him what I was. Am.

Rowan rolled onto his back, smiling in the dim light, the curve of his lips pushing his dimples in and crinkling the corner of his eye. "Not so much she was always right, but she knew *what* was right. Like ending the rifts between the clans. She'd been trying since she was a girl, apparently. It drove Father batty. He was very much the bespoke-suit-wearing Demon stereotype," he added softly. "Pain in my ass, but I miss him sometimes."

I held my tongue. The elder Hebert had been terrifying. A very old, very powerful Demon, one who remembered the days when Witches were tortured for being Witches and would speak of it with some fondness whenever one of us got too...whatever. But he'd also speak of his sons with such love and devotion it was like witnessing two different men. He had dozens of children scattered through the centuries, and he loved each and every one of them. He was proud of most, but not afraid or ashamed to speak against those who'd done awful things. And awful by Demon standards was perplexing.

"Grandma wanted this," Rowan said, though I don't know if it was to himself or to me. "She...she knew it had been too long, and the break was ridiculous and—" He turned his head to face me again. "Well. She and your grandmother were stubborn together."

I smiled. I missed Grandmere terribly, but the thought of her and Heliotrope together on the Other Side tickled me. "I pity the poor medium who contacts either one of them."

"Oh, gods. Can you imagine if they came through together?"

He laughed, a sudden burst of bright sound sending tiny sparks of pleasure through my entire body. The weird and fragile eggshell cracked a bit, letting some light in.

Or did it get firmer, keeping the bad out?

I was terrible with metaphors.

Rowan reached across the gap between our beds and grabbed the remote. "We're not watching this anyway." He turned off the movie.

"Hey! Maybe I was!"

"You were watching the hero's ass."

"...yeah, and?"

Rowan propped himself on his elbow and shot me a look I couldn't quite decipher. Or maybe I was too hesitant to decipher. Some mix of interest and amusement and...I gave up trying to pick it apart when he flopped back down on the bed. "We've got a long day tomorrow. We'd better get some sleep."

I nodded, turning off the light with a twist of my fingers from across the room.

Rowan sighed. "The Demons are wrong, you know. Witches are pretty useful."

I heard the smile in his voice but closed my eyes, not sure if I was hoping we'd fall asleep or stay up, unable to stop talking about nothing.

CHAPTER SEVEN

The holly and the ivy are giving me a rash

ROWAN

Nestled in a thick stand of bare-branched trees that would have been beautifully lush and less offensively green if the weather were warmer, the house was a neat little cottage, at home in any quaint English Faerie tale. Provided the Faerie tale involved a few doses of acid and one of those black light posters with a naked woman arched awkwardly over a mushroom or something. The only part of the house not acidly, virulently, painfully bright green was the shiny brass doorknob, gleaming sharply in the late morning sun.

"Rowan."

"Mmm?"

"I know I dozed off back there around the charming gas station with the doorless bathroom and the highly suspect gentleman selling jerky from the back of his van, but we're still in Arkansas, right? We didn't, I don't know, somehow veer off into whatever the hell place Willy Wonka lived?"

I shook my head, unable to look away from the house in front of us. "Definitely Arkansas. This is...a lot."

"I didn't know they made green paint in that particular shade."

"You mean 'offensively green'? Yeah, no, that's...that is definitely unique to this house."

"Offensively green might be putting it kindly," Whitaker murmured. "I may have retina damage."

"If you slowly move your head from side to side, the house leaves tracers."

Whitaker's phone vibrated in the cup holder like a horde of angry wasps, startling us both out of our verdant stupor. "Shit, it's Egon again."

He'd called so many times since we left the hotel I was starting to wonder if he had some weird fixation on Whitaker and was flailing out of jealousy. Biting down on that line of thought, I instead unbuckled and offered Whitaker a pained smile. "If you want to talk to him, I'll go in and do this real quick. It won't take long."

The phone rattled and buzzed again. Groaning, Whitaker closed his eyes, letting his head fall back against the seat. "It's more of the same," he admitted. "Nothing's changed at all. He's just..." He made a flapping gesture with his right hand.

"Yes, I see now where you get your reputation for being so suave and well-spoken."

"Hey, I'm off the clock. Put me in front of a Council session, and I'll suave and well-spoken your socks off."

I raised a brow. "Last time I saw you in front of a Council session, you talked my pants down, but I recall my socks staying on."

His cheeks turned a pretty pink, and he looked anywhere but at me for a moment, finally sliding me a side-eye glance. "Well. I wasn't in front of the Council when your, um, clothing malfunctioned. And if you'd have paid attention to your footwear during my turn at the head of the table, you'd have noticed your socks trying to slip off and wiggle away. It's a good thing you wore close-toed shoes." His blush deepened. "I've only had one cup of coffee, so I'm more ridiculous than usual." He caught the corner of his lower lip between his teeth, darting another glance my way and fiddling with the stitching on the steering wheel cover.

"You're a Witch sitting in a car with a Demon on a road trip to return some Yule ornaments your dead grandmother somehow accidentally shipped to mine, albeit a few years too late. I think we're beyond coffee's help when it comes to ridiculous things."

He gasped. "You take that back about coffee right this instant! How could you?!"

I couldn't help the inelegant snort. "No wonder Ellery thinks you're tolerable. He's practically got an altar to coffee in his kitchen."

"He thinks I'm tolerable? My heart's aflutter!" He pressed his palms against his chest and batted his lashes. "I might swoon!"

"Ugh," I muttered. "Worst Southern accent ever, by the bye. Keep it up, and I won't find you tolerable anymore."

Dropping his hands, Whitaker shifted to face me, his expression serious. "You think I'm just tolerable?"

"Are you seriously asking me?" It was my turn to blush. My face felt warm, and my neck prickled with the threat of nervous sweat, so of course, I knew I was looking super sexy right then as he stared at me from less than a foot away. "I find you...more than tolerable."

"Ah."

Damn it. That sound was both flat and low, a disappointed sigh more than an actual word. He didn't look upset so much as neutral. A mask.

I reached out tentatively for his arm and gave it a squeeze just below his bicep. "I thought you'd know by now I found you exceedingly more than tolerable." I didn't mean for my voice to pitch low, to come out in a soft growly way, but it did. Whitaker's eyes flashed wide and hot, just long enough for me to regret not giving in to that desire to kiss him the night before. I swayed towards him, and he tipped his head the tiniest bit to one side, his gaze on my mouth. I couldn't help the tiny tug of a smile making my lips quirk up. He huffed a put-upon sounding sigh, but his own expression was anything but annoyed. "Do you—"

The damn phone went off again, this time sounding, if possible, downright angry. Whitaker growled. Like, an actual, feral-sounding growl doing *things* for me.

"Talk to Egon," I sighed. "Let me go do this, and once I call Chloe with the information, we can get back on the road and make up some time."

He hesitated, then jerked his chin in a nod. Picking up his phone, he swiped to accept the call and frowned. "Damn it. The bars keep vanishing. I'm going down to the end of the drive and see if that helps. Are you sure you don't want me to come in with you?"

"Need? No. Want..." I let my gaze drift back to his lips again. "Want is something else entirely."

"Damn it."

"Get, before Egon does something weird and Witchy and summon you or something."

He made a face. "We can't do portals like Demons, you know. If he wanted me back fast, you'd have to do some Demon thing."

I affected an expression of innocence. "I wouldn't show my portal to just *any*one!" As he sputtered a laugh, I let myself out of the car. "See you in about fifteen or twenty," I called, heading for the lime-on-acid front door.

A single sprig of mistletoe was thumbtacked above the peephole. Upon inspection, it was plastic mistletoe. When I leaned in to examine the too-white berries, I realized it had been spritzed with pine-scented cleaner. Festive *and* germicidal.

I was hesitant to knock. The entire place had a distinctly muffled feel to it. Like trying to listen to the TV two rooms away with your head under a pillow. When no one answered, I craned my neck to see if I could spot Whitaker down the drive. No such luck; the drive had just enough of a curve and slope, making it impossible to see the road without having either exceptional vision or the neck of a giraffe. Trusting he hadn't decided to say fuck it and bail on me, I gave up trying to stalk him and knocked on the door again.

This time, it swung open almost immediately.

"Mr. Hebert."

"Yes." I plastered my work smile (the one Chloe said made her think I had a toothache or gas or both). "I'm here to see your armoire."

The Demon blinked—there was no mistaking one of my lot—and stood back, gesturing in a vaguely grand manner for me to come in. "Mrs. Greenbaum managed to track you down," they said in a breathless voice, the ragged edges of words making me wonder if they ran across the house to answer the door. I did my best not to gawk, but the place *was* enormous. Longer than it was wide, the house had a gallery construction, with doors opening off the central entry/corridor, which ran straight down the center of the house and terminated in a dark wood door at the far end.

As bright as the house was on the outside, inside, it was dark and smelled of mildew as only sodden plasterboard can smell. Threaded through the damp was the chemical odor of fake pine, like someone had given the floors a vigorous mopping with pine cleaner stuff. That couldn't be the case, I decided, as my shoes made a decidedly sticky sound when I took a step. "I'm sorry, Mrs. Greenbaum neglected to tell me your name," I said.

The Demon closed the door behind us, leaving us standing in the thin, gray-tinged light seeping in through the thick, dirty windows, and

stared at me for a long moment. "Are you sure you don't know my name, Mr. Hebert?"

Oh, good. Games. Demons, especially those of older generations, had a predisposition towards riddles, puzzles, scavenger hunts, Yahtzee... I admit to being really into Clue, but seriously, come on! It's Clue! How can someone *not* love that game?

Demons of older cohorts, though, they really loved the sort of ridiculous, infuriating contests you'd expect from a group who made its bread and butter being passive-aggressive: 'What do *you* think? Why do you think that? Where did you get that idea?' That sort of bullshit. Thankfully, my father had been a master at that sort of crap, and I knew how to deal with it.

By not dealing with it.

"Where is the armoire, then? I'd like to get the appraisal done and sent to my assistant before it gets much later. Mrs. Greenbaum wants to make arrangements for shipping as soon as possible."

They smiled thinly and headed down the central corridor, leaving me to follow. I had the dismal and honestly uncharitable thought that anyone living in a house like this wasn't likely to keep expensive antiques around, not when every little side table, bench, even the plaster plinth we'd passed was covered in thick dust and visible black mold. My guide glanced back over their shoulder, and something pinged at my mind, some sense of recognition or knowledge, but I couldn't place its origin.

The muffled sensation was thickest as we neared a door near the end of the corridor, on the left side. My host smiled, showing a row of tombstone teeth, and rapped twice on the door before pushing it open and standing aside once more. "In here," they said. "It's by the window."

"Uh, yeah, no." I folded my arms and stood back. "I watch enough of the I.D. channel to know not to turn my back on a stranger in their own house. You first." Honestly, being clonked on the back of the head and left to die wasn't really a worry. Even if the other Demon was stronger than me, taking me down would require more than simple assault. Still, it would hurt, and I was not into pain, either recreationally or incidentally.

The Demon hesitated for a tiny little flutter of a moment before tilting their head ever so slightly and smiling down at me. "It's merely a room, Mr. Hebert. A room and an armoire. But very well." They gave the door a nudge, and it swung open with a waft of mildew, damp plaster, and wet carpet. A thin thread of sulfur wove through the stench to really bring it all together.

Every alarm bell in my brain going off at once, full volume, I hesitated at the threshold. The Demon stood a few feet away, making an awkward gesture at a battered old armoire shining with a subtle silvery sheen, like someone had tried to make it appear old using wax and varnish. Four other Demons stood in a loose half-circle in front of it, like a community theater production of *The Crucible*.

"Oh, for fuck's sake." I took a chance and dropped into one of the suspicious armchairs dotting the room. I lucked out; it only *smelled* damp. It was, in fact, so dry the wood struts creaked in dismay, and fabric flaked off under my hand. "Have y'all never heard of a group chat? Or, I don't know, anything less dramatic?"

I wondered where Whitaker was; he would likely get a kick out of this mess. But then I thought better. If he was in the midst of this room full of typically reclusive, impatient Demons, it wouldn't matter whose son he was or what position he had in the Council, how powerful Whitaker's magic was or how well he could use it. A half-dozen very old Demons, none of whom cared much for Witches and still bemoaned the fact they were not allowed to *hunt* them, would see to it he met with some tragic, subtle end and tell everyone he died of natural causes.

I recognized half of the Demons by sight. They'd been...associates of my grandmother. *Friends* was far too strong of a word. The three eldest were trying their best not to look like they were awkwardly circling up for kindergarten story time, arms folded and feet shuffling.

"You would've ignored our concerns," said a tall, sallow, redhead I remembered from his afternoon visits on the first Friday of every month to the shop. River Paulson, a sourly unpleasant Demon of the old guard, one who liked to wear musty formal wear to meetings and insisted on drinking the most tannic tea possible and sneering at offers of sugar. And he was also blazingly douchey besides.

"Depending on what your concerns are, that's very likely, Mr. Paulson," I sighed. "I have somewhere I need to be, so let's hear it, and we can all leave dissatisfied and go on with our lives."

"Leo," Paulson snapped, waving his long hand towards the Demon who had been my tour guide of suck. "Check on the Witch. We need a minute."

Leo raised one pale brow. "Shall I...?"

Paulson exchanged glances with the others. "Best better had, just to be on the safe side."

"Better had what?" I demanded. Turning on one heel to follow Leo, the world lurched sideways for a nauseating second, and everything snapped in tight like a rubber band before relaxing. My breath caught in my chest and rattled until I could catch it. I stumbled back, hitting the edge of the low coffee table. I dropped to sit on it, ignoring the *tsk* from one of the assembled Demons. "Paulson—"

"Your association with the Frosts is pathetic," Paulson snapped. His lips drew back to bare his teeth, his entire face becoming skull-like, the skin pulled taut and eyes deeply shadowed. "While your grandmother lived, we tolerated it. She had standing in our community, despite her ways, and she was respected even in her eccentricity. You," he jabbed a long, waxy finger at me, "do not have our grace to behave like some sort of Witch's whore."

The strange contraction had left me dizzy and disoriented, but it faded enough for me to manage an award-worthy scowl. "Okay, I get it's in our blood to be dramatic fucks, but how did you even find out I was in Arkansas? And a Witch's whore? Seriously?"

I shoved myself to my feet with only a little wobble and tried to pass it off as a mocking bow. Judging by the sneer on Paulson's face, I'd either failed, or he'd caught a whiff of his upper lip.

"You've had every opportunity to have a say in our role in the Revelation plans." I waved a hand at Paulson and the other three Demons. I recognized Lucille Post, another one of Grandma's 'friends' (in that lovely Southern sense, in which the person might either be a friend or on Grandma's list of people to feed a laxative brownie to). She met my eyes and glanced away quickly, darting a look at Paulson before staring at some spot just over my left shoulder and adopting a half-assed sneer in my direction.

"You kept quiet," I went on. "Or not quiet, really. You did love to whisper behind backs and make oblique threats while doing absolute jack when it came time to make your feelings known."

"We made our feelings abundantly clear," Paulson snapped. "We told Heliotrope regularly. We submitted written statements to the Grand Council. When you shoved your way in as our ersatz representative, we demanded an audience with the heads of all the Demonborn clans and the Grand Council leaders."

That caught me across the chest. My breath stuttered as whatever I was about to say got tangled on my tongue and fell apart. My father had been head of our clan, but he'd died several years ago, not long after I started making a meaningful push for Demonborn representative on the Council. My oldest brother, Alastor, had become de facto head of our clan but had never mentioned anything about meetings with Paulson or anyone else, much less with the Grand Council leadership.

The Grand Council leadership which would have included Whitaker.

"Ah. Are you getting it now?" Paulson hissed. "He's using you. You're nothing but a toy for him. You'll bend over backward for that spoiled whelp of a Witch. You happily help them keep their place at the head of the table when they deserve *nothing*. They're nothing but jumped-up humans, stealing power from the Wellspring, abusing the knowledge our ancestors gave a precious few chosen servants!"

"Servants?" I shook my head, the woozy feeling returning slowly, creeping up from my stomach and settling in the base of my skull. "That's not what happened."

Paulson's lips finally pulled back over his teeth. He pursed them, giving Lucille Post a slight nod. She and the other two Demons spread out, murmuring softly. Too late, I realized what they were doing.

I lurched forward, trying to make it to the door in time, but I was stopped short and hard against an invisible wall of power. It sent me reeling back, sprawling on the floor as they finished their casting, and the circle was fully charged.

"You're not as subtle or clever as you think," Paulson said, crouching to meet my gaze from the other side of the sigil's faintly shimmering energetic field. "We sent Greenbaum to try one last time to make you see reason."

"One last time?" I scoffed. "Y'all haven't said a damn word to me since Grandma's funeral."

I got to my knees and had to stop for a moment, everything swimming unpleasantly like my eyes couldn't focus. *I'm not going to puke in front of them. That's all I need, hurling in front of these assholes.* I was already something of an outlier in the Demonborn community. Most of us didn't give two damns about the Revelation; Demons had been living amongst humans since before recorded human history. When we stopped being revered, stopped even being tolerated, we simply sank in. Not assimilated—we never tried to be *like* humans. We just...hid in plain sight. Alastor and Ellery always referred to it as using camouflage, relying on our outward resemblance to humans, hiding our communities amongst theirs.

A few Demons weren't content to keep existing in quiet, though. They wanted a return to our glory days (though, if they'd paid any attention to actual history, they'd know those days were rife with disease and politics gnawing away at us, human strife we took on as our own, nothing like the magical perfection they insisted was real). These Demons rumbled about the Revelation but never put up much of a fight. Mostly because they were so few in number. But also because...

My thoughts ground to a halt. Because *why*?

I looked back up at Paulson, who was studying me with a naked curiosity that made me feel like a lab specimen. "How did you know where I'd be?"

"Devil's own luck," he chuckled. "Regina Greenbaum was to make one final attempt at contact. Heliotrope had blocked us for years, refusing all meetings. Your own father had humored her and your mother..." He trailed off, unable to keep from rolling his eyes.

"Yeah, I get that," I sighed. Eye rolls were pretty much SOP when it came to dealing with my mother.

"Since you've been stirring the cauldron," he tittered at his own joke, "we knew it was time for one last push, and if that didn't work, then we had no other option." He rose, his knees popping and creaking as he stretched to his full height. "Regina stopped by the shop two days ago. Your assistant mentioned you were going on a bit of a trip. She's a chatterbox. Couldn't wait to ask Regina about her spoon collection and if she had one from Arkansas because you were hoping to complete your collection while you were driving through the state."

Shit. Goddamn it, Chloe.

"So, you set up a Scooby Doo trap to make me hear you out?"

He smiled. What may have been a charming expression on a different person was cadaverous on Paulson. "The Witches aren't exactly subtle, are they? Especially when they feel slighted. They've been screeching to whoever would listen about how you've managed to steal their silver bells. We were pleased." He nodded towards Lucille Post and the other two Demons. "Until we realized the rumors of a Frost in the area were true. And you were stuck to him like shit on a shoe."

I finally managed to get to my feet, the nausea abated enough so I could move without imminent danger of my breakfast reappearing. The four Demons had all moved together towards the door, standing two on each side. Waiting.

Fuck.

"So you decided to trap us here for what purpose? We don't get to where we need to be, people will look for us."

Yeah, I know. Most trite response to a kidnapping ever. Still...it was true.

"Yes. They will look for you. The Demon who they think stole their sacred silver bells. The bells allowing them to tap into power that was never rightfully theirs. They'll look for the Demon they think is capable of stealing their link to the Wellspring, the Demon that disappeared with their brat."

Hearing anyone refer to Whitaker as a terror was enough to make me stifle a laugh. He was a grown man (very grown, thank you very much) and the furthest thing from a spoiled brat I could imagine. But...but I could see what was unfolding now. "And this is a ham-handed frame-job?" I asked as archly as I could manage. "Make them think I kidnapped him?"

"No. Make them think you killed him."

CHAPTER EIGHT

D*o you see what I see?*

WHITAKER

"This is unacceptable, Whitaker. You're well aware of the Council's position on including Demons in the proceedings."

The thrumming headache behind my right eye increased its tempo from a steady march into something closer to the musical stylings of a washing machine full of sneakers. "You didn't protest when we made the agreement with Simon Detweiler a few months ago," I began, only to have Egon cut me off with a wet-sounding snort.

Gross.

"The situation with the *changeling*," he inflected the word with a theatrical amount of disdain, "was exceptional. The situation with your pet Demon is in poor taste. Your grandmother, rest her soul, was a unique woman, and despite her rather *outré* views, she was a very respected and powerful member of our community. But—"

"But," I said, not even bothering to temper my tone, "Rowan Hebert isn't anyone's pet. He's been working on behalf of the Demonborn for years. Grandmere saw in him a kindred spirit and felt it was not only a good idea but vital to the Revelation to have the Demonborn are counted with us."

Egon was quiet for a long, tooth-grindingly loud moment. "Your grandmother was a very special woman," he said finally in a tone meant to be pleasant but one any person who spent even a little bit of time in the South could tell you meant *fuck off and die in a fire*. "Madam Frost was a valuable part of the Council and had a tremendous amount of influence. But some of her opinions were less than favorable for our cause."

"Less than favorable opinions are things like mustard belongs in potato salad, or Mega Bloks are better than LEGO. Believing Demonborn should have a place in the Council and a say in things as we go forward isn't an opinion, Egon. It's common sense." I could practically hear my mother's tongue clicking disapprovingly at my tone. "Her wishes were clear, explicitly stated in her will and in the Council minutes."

Egon sighed softly, a tiny sound full of regret that I knew, in my heart of hearts, had to be manufactured. "Whitaker, we've discussed this before. Her will has no sway over the Council, nor does whatever she said in the meetings. In fact, it is in the best interests of the Council if such trifles are forgotten. They only serve to cause tension and dissension amongst the members, something we cannot afford this close to the Revelation." He made a satisfied smacking noise, like the very idea tasted good on his tongue. "It's best for everyone if members who wantonly delay our forward progress or seek to derail it are removed from proceedings. We're too close to our goal now."

Anger slid down the back of my neck like a snake, warm and strong and slick. It settled, coiled at the base of my spine, and tightened until my gut ached with it. "Are you threatening me, Egon?"

His pause was genuine, not just for effect. "Pardon?"

"As a Council member, one who has openly taken up my grandmother's work and is advocating for the inclusion of Demonborn in this process, even if it means delaying it by another year," I didn't add *or more*, but I was pretty sure it was implied, judging by the snarl on Egon's end of the line, "I am one of the people you wish to...what was that? Remove from proceedings?" It was my turn to click my tongue, doing my best not to think about how, oh gods, I might be turning into my mother. "I don't mean to stroke my own ego here, Egon, but I'd think removing me from the Council would upset more than a few apple carts. I mean, the Frosts are the oldest Witch clan in the States. With Grandmere's passing, I'm the head of the clan. Kicking me off the Council would be bad optics, wouldn't it? Especially at the Solstice when we're gathered at the Frost family home for the ceremony."

Egon's breathing was loud and raspy. I wondered if he'd handed the phone off to one of his dogs. "You know damn well that's not what I meant."

I glanced back at the house and startled. The front door was open, and a tall, gaunt person was standing on the front porch, hands folded in front of them, staring at me like a suburban Nosferatu cosplayer, all gray and black and white but in front of a Craftsman instead of a rickety castle. "We'll talk later, Egon."

"I have concerns about your association with Rowan Hebert. Many on the Council feel he—"

Yes, I hung up. No, it wasn't the most mature thing to do. But between sheer exhaustion with Egon's bigotry and the weird stare I was getting from Tall, Pale, and Creepy, I had zero patience left.

"Hi?" I called, walking a few feet down the drive. A fuzzy, prickly sensation raced over my skin like static electricity but deeper, somehow. My own magic perked up, stretching towards whatever was moving along my aura. The angry snake coiled powerfully in my spine slithered away, replaced by a bevy of uncertain spiders all jittering nervously.

Seriously. If you've ever been in a situation like that one, you'd agree it feels like you're full of anxious arachnids. Trust me on this one.

The person on the porch didn't move.

"I'm just waiting on Rowan. Er, Mr. Hebert." I tried a smile, one of those small and polite ones people use when they are trying not to look suspicious.

They just stared.

The prickly, tingly feeling increased. It was damn near painful, a combination of electricity and ripping a bandage off one arm hair at a time. Definitely Demon. I'd entertained the thought the person might be a vampire, but there were so few in the world and none of them in Arkansas, so I'd dismissed the notion before it even took root. They were definitely not a Witch, or Fae, or even a half-born. This one was a Demon, through and through.

The fizz-spark of Demon magic raced over me again, smarting enough to make my eyes water before suddenly releasing. I felt weirdly bereft, like the magic took something with it when the Demon pulled back. Despite what Witches had to do at the Solstice to maintain our ties to the Wellspring, we were never truly powerless. Our histories told of Witches forced out of clans or cut off somehow who became so removed from their powers that they just stopped living. Nothing dramatic so much as withered away. They lived less, slowly emptying of will until they simply...weren't anymore. Even though it wasn't a common occurrence, and, as punishments went, being exiled was extreme and rare (I couldn't even remember the last time it had happened, something relegated to a history lesson and a vague bogeyman story for little Witches everywhere), I had a moment of panic when the feeling something had been taken from me pinged.

The Demon moved, a subtle twitch of the lips, and finally turned to go back into the house. I found my voice and called after them. "Hey! Hey, wait! Is—"

The door shut before I could move more than a few feet towards the front steps.

Shit.

I glanced at my phone to check the time, half-expecting to see a text notification from Egon waiting. There was one, but it was from an unknown number. I glanced back up at the house, expecting...I don't know what. A sign from Rowan? Something Demonic and fiery maybe? Or a sign in the window? I tapped my fingers against my thigh, restlessness seeping into my body, replacing the weird twinge of loss.

Maybe, I thought, it was some Demon charm. The Demons who used such things had dozens, if not hundreds, at their ready disposal, things to make people feel any sort of way. Such charms allegedly didn't last long, but they were strong on regular humans and had been used by less-than-scrupulous Demons over the centuries to manipulate and contrive.

Still, to be on the safe side, I gave my powers a wiggle. Nothing huge and flashy. Just sort of a systems check to make sure the engine was still humming and all pistons were firing or some other automotive metaphor, terribly butch and apropos for the situation.

Nothing *seemed* missing. I was even able to dredge up an old childhood skill I'd learned from my Uncle Andronicus and manage a bit of conversation with a rather chilly and annoyed squirrel displeased I was lurking under his tree. Still, I couldn't shake the feeling. A stiff breeze rattled its way through the scattering of leafless trees in the front yard, a bitter ribbon of wind cutting through the damp chill and reminding me just how close to the Solstice we were, snapping me out of my rumination. Rowan still wasn't out yet, nearly an hour after he'd gone inside.

"Fuck," I muttered. The car would be nice and warm, and I could take a short nap while I waited. But we needed to get back on the road, and taking a short nap inevitably meant sleeping for way longer than planned. Frankly, I didn't think I could face ten hours on the road with a Bad Decision Nap hangover and Rowan being all...Rowany, with his rumpled hotness and snark and that thing he did with his tongue when he was thinking and...

Fuck.

First stop on the way out of town would be for coffee. A quick devotion to Caffeina the Great would scrape some of the fuzz off my thoughts and get my head back in the game.

Hopefully.

The squirrel chittered angrily again from his spot in a deep knothole in a nearby oak.

"Nobody asked you."

Considering my options, I paced back to the car. Waiting in the car meant I'd likely doze off, which was not a great idea at the moment. Even with warding spells set, my lack of consciousness might mean they'd slip. Even powerful Witches like Grandmere couldn't keep warding spells at full strength while they slept. That required specialized charm-work and tools I didn't have access to on this little road trip side jaunt.

My other option was knocking on the door and demanding Rowan hurry the Hell up.

Though, a tiny voice nudged, I was fairly certain he wasn't taking so long out of his own volition. Something was wrong, and the longer I waited, the wronger it'd get.

More wrong? Wronger? Wronging?

Eh, it'd be worse.

In either scenario, there was also the problem of the bells. I couldn't leave them unprotected in the car while I went into the house, I couldn't carry them with me into a potentially dangerous situation, and I couldn't risk dozing off and someone managing to take them.

Who would take them? No idea. But they'd gone missing once already, so why chance it again?

I growled under my breath and tipped my face up to the steely clouds overhead, heavy with icy rain threatening to fall. The squirrel chittered again, rapid-fire and sharp, underscoring his point by chucking a half-chewed pine cone at my head. "Hey!" He fluffed his tail at me from the crotch of the old tree, deep in the vee of the branches before disappearing deep inside the hollow.

Oh.

Okay.

IT TOOK A GRAND TOTAL of ten knocks, increasing exponentially in volume (with, admittedly, a tiny bit of help from an easy charm most Witches learned as kids, amplifying sound enough to be irritating without making ears bleed or setting off car alarms) before Tall, Pale, and Creepy opened the door.

"I'm waiting for Mr. Hebert," I said before they could speak.

They just continued staring at me in that *I bet you'd make a lovely vest and pair of slippers* kind of way, quiet and intimidating.

They didn't even blink as they pushed a squirming tendril of Demonborn power at me, no doubt intending to intimidate me, maybe even make me leave. It was uncomfortable—crackling and hot as it sizzled through me—but harmless. A warning shot across the bow.

"Look," I sighed as they withdrew their questing little tentacle of power, "we both know he's in there, unless he decided to sneak out the back window and hitchhike to...well. Hitchhike. Let's cut the Nosferatu cosplay crap and either tell him I'm here or let me go get him."

They stared for another long moment. When they spoke, it was startling. A sudden burst of sound where there'd only been quiet mere seconds before. I honestly had not expected them to say anything, only show me where Rowan was. Or burst into a flurry of bats or something. "Mr. Hebert is in a meeting. You may wait in the foyer but go no further."

They stepped back, lifting one languid hand to indicate a midcentury padded bench upholstered in a highly offensive shade of mustard yellow, tucked up against a wall papered in a mirrored sixties toile print. Any taste involved in decorating had been entirely within the mouth of the decorator. The only thing not straight out of the Brady Bunch's rummage sale was the floor. Thickly varnished dark wood, inscribed with swirling, interlocking sigils. They were difficult to see unless you squinted, tilted your head just right, and the light was perfect, but the stars aligned for me. When I sighed and let my head roll to one side while Lurch-Lite fussed over a dusty vase of flocked plastic roses near a set of double doors, I spotted them.

They were scratched in and, in a few cases, burned lightly into the wood, like someone had let an iron rest a second too long but rescued it before it could start the wood aflame. I didn't recognize the symbols, beyond knowing they were Demon magic. Even if I'd known them, I lacked the ability to use them. It wasn't so much that the Demons kept their magic close to the chest but it was so specific to them, so ingrained in their very beings, that anyone not of their kind could never hope to use it.

While Fae and Witches had some overlap in powers, Demon magic, true Demon magic, was in a world of its own. Stories said Demons had, at one point, taught humans things like artifice and weapon making, mundanities like living in the wild and thriving, as well as miraculous things, like using certain plants to heal and others to harm. And once, maybe twice or three times, Demons had favored a human. A human Demons loved enough to bring them into the fold and teach them small and tentative magics humans could handle.

When the first Witches were made, that handful of humans already open to magic, able to See and Hear things no others could, Demonborn were there to teach Witches how to fold nature with a pinch of the fingers, pluck the ephemeral from the air and make it real.

And over the centuries, Witches pretended not to remember where they'd learned it. Hell, a lot of us didn't remember or tried to pretend they didn't. And Witches had been determined, as a group anyway, to make sure any ties to Demonborn were kept buried deep.

Fun.

My erstwhile host loomed over me, baring their teeth in a too-white smile. "Are you a good Witch or a bad Witch?"

"Seriously?" It startled a laugh out of me, barking loud and unsettled.

"I mean," they said in a singsong kind of voice. They took up a perch next to me on the bench from the Brady Bunch yard sale, folding those spidery limbs into an approximation of polite interest. "Are you a Witch that believes Demons are equal, if not greater, to you, or are you a Witch that believes Demons and their role in your very existence should be quelled?"

They asked it in such a soft, rolling cadence, such a sweet-sounding tone. For a moment, I didn't realize what they were asking me. The urge to ask *don't you know who I am* was strong, my inner Dudebro rising up and trying to take charge of the encounter.

Bad Chad. Down, boy.

Instead, I plastered my polite client encounter smile on my face and widened my eyes a bit. "Why would I be traveling with Mr. Hebert if I thought Demons were beneath me?"

"Have you heard of the phrase 'useful idiot?'"

"Wow. That's pretty reductive and a slur to boot."

They rolled their eyes. "Don't attempt disingenuity with me, Witch Frost."

Oh, yikes. This Demon was an old one, or was mimicking the old formalities, anyway. "So you know who I am. Then you know my stance on Demons in the Council and—"

"And," they said flatly, "I know you are a Witch." Rising, they held out one hand towards me, palm out and fingers spread. That sensation of something being pulled loose washed through me again, leaving me nauseated. Glancing back down the hall towards a closed set of double doors, the Demon smiled faintly and nodded. "Come with me," they said sharply. "They are ready."

Crap. I was being taken to a secondary location. I'd heard how this turned out. I watched Crime T.V. "I'll wait here." I feigned a (ha) devil-may-care attitude. I stretched my legs in front of me and crossed them at the ankle, clasping my hands across my middle.

The Demon's brows scrunched together, and their lips thinned to a bare slit in their face.

"What," they demanded, eyes sweeping over me, "are you doing?"

"Waiting for Mr. Hebert." I pressed my hand against my solar plexus firmly but subtly. Or I hoped it was subtle. It wouldn't take much to pull the energy to the surface, just a bit of concentration and a willingness to let it go when the time came. The Demon's lips made a reappearance in the form of a wide, very fake smile.

"Let me take you to him," they said cheerfully. "Just here." Their hand shot out, and they breathed a word in a language I'd never heard. A hot, rolling wash of nausea crashed over me, making me gasp and lurch forward. I lost track of the fetch I'd been trying to call forth as the Demon muttered another word, and my limbs went weak.

CHAPTER NINE

W*hitaker feels like he got run over by a reindeer*

ROWAN

Whitaker lurched into the room, followed by the Demon who had been acting as Paulson's butler, apparently.

"Demaris," Paulson snapped, motioning for one of the lookalike Demons to come forward. The slightly shorter of the two strode to Whitaker's side in a few steps and grabbed his hand, pricking him with a small black blade. Whitaker gasped and jerked back, but the Demon who'd led him in blocked him, making him bounce back towards Paulson. Demaris and his compatriot pushed the coffee table out of the way, joined by Lucille Post.

I didn't have to hear the chanting to know what they were doing. "We're not like this anymore," I warned Paulson. "Even my father wouldn't have condoned this, and you *know* how he felt about Witches."

"Your father is dead," Paulson reminded me. "And your brother refuses to take the reins as he should. Your clan is withering, Rowan Hebert, and weak. Your branch will be pruned," he added with a sharp click of his teeth, a snapping bite more unsettling than I would have imagined. "Ellery has taken up with that anathema, simpering and slavering over him and bringing shame to the Circle. Alastor refuses to take his position and brings disgrace to your family in his refusal. And you..."

He bent low to peer into my eyes while I knelt in that damned circle. "You are a Witch's whore. You debase yourself for this creature."

He swung his arm to point at Whitaker, who was waxy pale and sweating. The fuzz-snap of magic in the room was uncomfortable for me, so I could only imagine how painful it was for Whitaker, unused to Demon magic as he was. A little zing here and there, a touch of fire or a miracle of snow was nothing. Magic borrowed from the elements around us. Harnessing nature in an ancient way, reaching past whatever barrier blocked humans from doing it and pulling on a few threads to make nature cooperate with our desires.

But this? The black knife? The sigils? The shedding of blood into the circle, which Demaris and his shadow were doing with Lucille Post? This was beyond elemental trickery. This was *old*. This was power that Witches would never tap into, weren't meant to tap into.

"You," Paulson snarled, "you know what Witches have taken from us, yet you persist in forcing our necks to bend for them."

"All I've done is try to make sure we have a seat at the table." I knew it was useless to argue with Paulson and others like him, but I couldn't stop the words from coming out of my mouth. Whitaker leaned heavily against Nosferatu-Wannabe, visibly shaking now. "What did you do to him?"

"The oldest ways are often the best," Paulson said, his grin slipping from manic-sharp to confidently smug. At a nod from Paulson, Whitaker's keeper held out his own left hand and opened his fingers. Two small orbs lay in his palm. As I stared, one shot up into the air and through the ceiling. Whitaker made a soft keening sound and closed his eyes, slumping in the Demon's grip. The other orb rolled in his palm like a marble before swizzling upwards much more slowly than the first one. Drifting like dandelion fluff towards the window, it bounced off a few times before melting through and into the daylight on the other side.

The circle being prepared next to mine was glowing a virulent shade of blue, one reminding me of the sigils my father used to pass Between. "Now," Paulson said shortly.

The Demon holding Whitaker shoved him forward, and he fell, sprawling face-first into the circle. Demaris shook the knife, scattering the drops of blood from the blade into the sigil. The glow bloomed, rushing like fire over Whitaker.

I shouted, screaming every countercharm and old magic I knew. Blocking, breaking, everything Father had ever taught us. I tore at the magic with my own, battering against it like a moth against a bulb. It drained me, pulling on my power, making me realize belatedly I was only making it stronger. Whatever I threw at it was being pulled in and turned for its own benefit.

I choked down the words. I pulled in my magic. *Shit.* I had to think, but I had no idea what to do next.

Whitaker pushed himself onto all fours, bleary-eyed and swaying. He raised his head to find me and offered me a jagged, unhappy smile.

"Bits of life force," Paulson said.

"My fetch," Whitaker corrected. He tried to wink at me, I was fairly sure, but managed to look about to vomit.

Though, to be fair, both things were probably true.

"You're going to kill both of us," I said slowly, the words weird and heavy on my tongue. "This is really fucking arcane, even for Demons. It would have been easier just to, I don't know, run us off the road somewhere. Shoot us and make it look like a murder-suicide."

Whitaker groaned, rolling to sit spraddle-legged in the middle of the sigil. "Maybe you should stop giving them ideas, in case this doesn't work out."

"Sorry. I meant, you could have just sent us to stay at a five-star resort in the Seychelles. Ooooh, that'd be so awful. Or worse, maybe given us a million dollars tax-free and a lifetime supply of our favorite foods. That'd really teach us a lesson."

Whitaker wheezed. I chose to believe it was a laugh.

Paulson rolled his eyes. "Miss Post, Demaris, Ramey, with me. Lowery, you know how to reach us when it begins."

Lowery, who I would always think of as Nosferatu's uglier stunt double, nodded eagerly. "Of course. If I may ask..."

"Sooner than they think." Paulson smiled. "The Witches should know about Witch Frost's sad demise at the hands of one he considered a friend. When they come, you can release Hebert from his circle. But not too soon, hm?" He slapped Lowery on the back, motioned to the others, and swept out in a cloud of self-righteousness.

Asshole.

Lowery backed out of the room and closed the door gently behind him, leaving Whitaker and I in our respective circles. I let out a shuddering, aching breath and turned my attention to Whitaker, hoping to assess whatever damage had been done to start figuring out a way out of our little prisons. My stomach cramped with the bowel-liquidating variety of fear, making me glad I'd skipped breakfast but sorry I'd opted for coffee instead.

"Whitaker," I said quietly, not sure if we had an audience on the other side of the doors or not. "Whitaker, I don't know what exactly they made here, but—"

"Jesus, are all Demons that annoying? I mean, that specific brand of mystic woo woo irritating?" Whitaker was sitting up straight, still pale but not as sick-looking as minutes before. He offered me a small, tired smile. "Tell me that this," he flicked his fingers at the circle around him, "is breakable."

"Yes," I said slowly, "but not by me. I tried when they were shoving you in here, but all it did was make the magic stronger. Um, quick question—what the fuck?"

"Hm? Oh, I faked most of it."

"Follow-up question. Why the fuck?"

"Survival instinct," he chuckled weakly. "Lurch's stunt double out there hit me with something that made me feel sick, but I was in the middle of pulling up my fetch." He darted a glance my way. "That sounds dirtier than it should."

"I was gonna let that one go, given the circumstances," I said, smiling back just a little.

"Whatever they hit me with didn't do as much damage as I think it was meant to."

"And your fetch..." I thought of the little orbs Paulson had taken earlier. "Did they..."

Whitaker groaned softly and shook his head. Quietly, quickly, he told me about his encounter with Discount Oddjob outside, the weird sensation something had been taken away, then the same feeling when Paulson had taken hold of him. "I don't know what they were looking for, but when I felt that pull again, I pushed my fetch out. I was hoping..." He sighed. "It's difficult to control without the anchoring I showed you last night. Hell, I'm glad I thought of doing that ritual last night. I can't say I would've even considered my fetch if it hadn't been so fresh in my mind." He shifted, uncomfortable in his expensive jeans and too-nice-for-a-road trip sweater. "Gotta be honest, not a hundred percent sure what I was hoping to do with it, but I thought maybe I could send for help or something."

"Like...Lassie?" I whistled. "Fetch, c'mere boy! C'mon, Fetch! Rowan and Whitaker have been taken captive by a bunch of shit-stain Demon supremacists! Here boy!"

"Ah," Whitaker sighed. "Care to expand on that?"

I scrubbed my hands over my face, feeling the grit and grime of everything settling over me as I told him Paulson's plan. "I have a theory," I said afterward, "that being non-human somehow means we have the Scooby Doo villain gene, but it's not active in all of us."

Whitaker snorted. "That might explain some things." He reached out and touched the faint glow of the circle, jerking his hand back with a sharp hiss. "Fuck!" His curse was followed by a soft, pained gasp. "Oh. Okay, yeah, that was a bad idea." He shuddered, then slumped floor-wards "I'm gonna...just lay down a minute," he said, stretching out. Within seconds, he was snoring softly.

That...was definitely not ideal.

I didn't know how much time passed before Whitaker stirred. My phone was dead as a doornail—not a surprise considering how much magic was saturating the room. The human myth about ghosts draining batteries and such wasn't entirely wrong; supernatural energy was not compatible with 4G coverage. Or most electronics, if you're not careful. The house was silent, but it didn't feel like we were alone. Lowery hadn't made an appearance since Paulson left, but that didn't mean anything.

Deciding maybe Whitaker had the right idea, I groaned and stretched out on the dusty floor facing the damned armoire. "Just for the record," I told it, "I don't care if you've got fucking Narnia hidden in there. I'm burning you to cinders once we're out of here."

A soft laugh sounded near my ear. It sounded like Whitaker but smaller, breathier. I rolled onto my back, confronted with a small orb about the size of a pea, faintly green and pulsing just enough to make my eyes want to cross. "Oh, hey," I said, drawing the word out like I was talking to a really skittish puppy. "How are you?"

If a fetch could give the stink eye...

"You need to get back to Whitaker," I said. It bounced once. "Was that a yes?" *Bounce.* "Um, he's not gonna die without you, right?" *Bounce bounce.* "Is that double yes? Or a no?"

It stared. Well, I assume, if it had eyes, it would have stared. It hung there in the air, pulsing slowly as if in time with Whitaker's sleeping breaths.

"Okay. So. You're part of him. He sent you out last night..." The orb dropped an inch or so until it was even with my eyes. I had the feeling it was glaring now. "Right, okay, yes. You're a tiny part of him, and you can't get back to him because of the sigil. You're not strong enough to stay apart too long, though." Something Whitaker said the night before sprang up and waved in my thoughts. "You're him," I said slowly. "So...okay, can you do something if I ask?"

It wobbled. I decided that meant *Well, I wouldn't normally, but since it's you asking...sure.*

"I CAN'T UNTANGLE THEIR layers of spell-work," I admitted. "I tried a few things, but it just seemed to make the damn thing stronger."

Alastor wavered in the blue glow of his sigil. The room had been so crowded and over-layered with magic; he hadn't been able to open a portal wide enough to move Between. Instead, he was...well, wherever he was, frowning at the janky study through the shine of a half-open portal, unable to touch anything but able to see and hear me just fine. "Without being there, I can't even begin to tell you what they've made, but based on your description, it sounds a bit like one of the old spells our ancestors used to protect sacred spaces."

"Uh..."

He rolled his eyes. "Back when humans thought we were the bee's knees and built us temples to live in? Entrapment spells? Fuck's sake, Ro, did you sleep through every Saturday school session or just the ones Father taught?"

"I didn't sleep through them! I've just recompartmentalized the information since then!"

I totally slept through them. Saturday school, the bane of every Demon child's existence from age five to seventeen, where we learned our history, our traditions, our...well. We learned a lot of stuff, and most of it was really boring when taught by doddering old Demons in sweater sets smelling of mothballs.

Whitaker shifted in his sleep, his breathing slow and ponderous. "This," I pointed at him, "isn't normal, Alastor. He's sleeping like he's drugged."

"Not drugged. Drained. His blood is powering the circle, from the sound of things." Alastor leaned forward, as if he could get a closer look at the sigil from that vantage point." The faint pinprick of Whitaker's fetch hovered near Whitaker himself, as close as it could get to the barrier without touching it. It wanted, needed, to go back to the source, and I worried it was going to be too weak or even gone entirely by the time we got the damned spell broken.

"Demon magic," Alastor said slowly, softly, as if he were talking to himself, "is very different from Witch magic, despite coming from the same source. Rather, Witch magic comes from a source Demons can access, but our magic itself is part of us, woven in our cells from the moment the first stars spat us out."

His smile twisted into a wry expression that looked so much like Father, I nearly choked on my own breath.

"Basically, they're not built to handle our magic This," he waved one finger at the situation Whitaker was in, "is very old magic, something Demons don't generally do anymore since it is far more paperwork than it's worth once the shit hits the fan and a tribunal is called." He *tsked*. "Seriously. Even the most anti-Revelation Demon in the Circle is going to demand a tribunal over this. This is what zealotry will get you, you know. Poorly executed plans and a court date to be determined later."

Oh, gods. He was pontificating. If I didn't nip that in the bud pronto, he'd go on for ages, and I'd be killed on a gross study floor while Alastor rambled on about the responsibilities of power or something. "Alastor. Brother dearest. The eldest and most responsible of us all."

"Hm. Right. Well. As this is some version of a very old magic, there's not much I can do without something to either physically cut the sigil, like Father's old obsidian blade from Uncle Asmodeus, or..." He *hmmed* again. "Well, the simplest thing to try would be to clean up the blood spill."

"And how would I do that?" I demanded, my patience down to one tiny, frayed fiber that had seen much better days. "I'm just as stuck as he is."

Alastor's sigh this time was every inch aggrieved elder brother. "Are you, though?"

I made a wide-eyed *well, duh* face and reached out to touch the barrier while staring at Alastor. It popped and pulsed, making me grunt in pain. "That's a big ol' yes."

"You, in the words of Anne Shirley, lack scope."

When he didn't expand, it was my turn to roll my eyes. "If you're waiting for me to have some sort of a grand revelation, it's not gonna happen, Alastor. I'm starving, need to pee like a cow on a flat rock, and, oh yeah, Whitaker Frost is dying four feet away from me, so you might have to connect some dots for me here because I am stressed the fuck out!"

"You're a Demon," he sighed. "And not a weak one. You are your father's son."

"Less cryptic, Nostradamus."

"For fuck's sake, make your own damn portal within your sigil, numb nuts." Alastor's own eyes went wide then, and he cleared his throat. "That should work. You're merely trapped, to be released when the Witches send someone for Whitaker, yes? Then you should be able to create a portal and move Between."

I stood shakily, a hot wash of nervous embarrassment creeping down my throat. "If you're telling me I've been sitting here for *hours* when I could've gotten out any time..."

Alastor smiled. "I'll give you a moment, shall I?" he asked before turning his face to give me a bit of privacy while I fumbled my way through a portal incantation. When it finally opened, a rush of power coursed in my veins, the gleeful pulse of *yes mine* chasing it.

Opening a portal like this was a thrill beyond anything else I'd ever felt. Between the magic, endorphins, and the ineffable knowledge I was a being of no small power, I understood, at least a tiny bit, people who thought Demons were more powerful than any other being.

I stepped through the portal and felt myself pulled in every direction at once, my atoms threatening to spread across the universe and leave my soul behind. The sensation lasted an eternal second before I snapped together like two magnets, unpleasant but not painful. I stepped out of the opening and into the gross study. The sudden lack of magical barrier around me was disorienting for a breath or two.

Alastor clapped once. "Good man," he cheered. "Now clean the blood splatter and see how that works out."

The blood, only a few drops really, was already dried on the dusty wood floor. I knelt and gingerly touched the nearest drop, brushing the barrier around Whitaker. It drew on my power, tiny suction cups pulling on my essence, but I got to work. I scraped with my thumbnail as the barrier pulsed and thickened. After the third droplet, it shuddered.

Magic had no feelings. Magic gave zero fucks about you, me, or anyone I knew. But it seemed that the barrier, the magic they'd used to trap Whitaker, was anxious, angry even, as I removed more of his blood. By the time I reached the last droplet, the barrier was finally thinning, but the anxious feeling remained.

"Now," Alastor said, startling me. I'd forgotten he was there for several moments, and his voice was loud in the quiet room. "Stand back."

I scooted back. The tiny, barely there flicker of a fetch drifted lazily past and drooped down towards Whitaker like dandelion fluff. It faded against the dark tones of his hair, and I worried, for a moment, it had flickered out of existence entirely.

"That little trick was quite ingenious," Alastor murmured as we waited. "I feel a bit bad for how long it took me to notice the poor thing, but, to be fair, I was in the middle of an interview with a new rigging team, and I thought it was just some glare off the equipment." He sighed. "I'm getting old."

Whitaker's breathing was less labored after a few moments, but he still wasn't waking. "I'm not sure what to do," I admitted. "We...um. We're supposed to take these bells..."

Alastor groaned. "I'd heard," he admitted. "Chloe."

"She's so fired," I sighed. "She can't keep quiet about anything."

"To be fair," Alastor begin, but a loud bang somewhere in the house made us both still. "Well. I'll let you get to it then."

"Alastor—"

"We'll talk after Solstice," he said firmly. "About all of this."

"Wait! I—" The portal closed, and he was gone.

There was another bang, then a loud scraping noise. Someone moving something heavy. I wished the fetch was back because I felt terribly alone just then. "Whitaker," I muttered. "Now would be a great time to wake up." I swept my hand through the circle and felt only the faintest tingle of magic. For all intents and purposes, it was gone. "Come on, come on, come on..."

The door swung open, and Paulson was there, Lucille Post at his side. She looked frazzled, far older than she had that morning and too soft around the edges, like she was losing definition under pressure. "Did you think we didn't have wards set to tell us if you managed to escape?" Paulson demanded.

Here we go. "I'd hoped maybe you hadn't gone full cartoon villain, but here we are," I said with a disappointed shake of my head. "Now, let us leave, or I'll kill you."

Paulson snorted over Lucille's squeak. "You have never taken a life, Rowan, and I doubt you'll start today." He swept into the room, heading straight for me. I jumped to my feet and threw both hands out. A wall of fire swept over Paulson, making him stop long enough for me to get out of swinging range. Paulson growled a string of obscenities and reached for me again as I danced back. "Lucille! Doors!"

She nodded, eyes watery and wide, but did as she was told.

"Miss Post," I said, throwing out my hands again to block Paulson's blast of magic. "Do you remember when you taught my Saturday school class? I was in seventh grade. You were filling in for Grandma. She had the flu."

Lucille Post nodded. "Y...yes. Yes, I remember."

"You were her friend."

"We...we weren't close. But yes."

"Oh, for..." Paulson spat an incantation, and a shelf full of books tore away from the wall and flew at me. They missed me, but a few winged Lucille right on the arm.

"You were her friend, Miss Post. Are you going to let me be killed just because you disagree with me? You'd stand by while your friend's grandson is murdered?"

She started to shake her head but caught Paulson's eye and shook it. "I can't, Rowan. You don't understand. If we allow them to dictate what we can and can't do, how we live our lives..." She made a helpless gesture. "Your grandmother didn't know humans like I do. Like we do. We've been Seen before, a lot of us. Back before you were born. And being Seen got so many of us killed, or worse."

I dropped my hands. Paulson made a soft noise of triumph and started towards me again. I shoved the coffee table at him, kneecapping him and getting him out of the way for a moment. "That's not what this is, Miss Post. It isn't about giving up ourselves."

"Isn't it?" she asked softly. "If we're part of this Revelation, we have to give up everything in order to stay safe. We'll have to live how humans want us to live. We'll lose everything and be called liars and worse. What about Demons married to humans, who have babies with humans, and their partners don't know? How will this affect them, hm?" She shook her head again. "I can't let anyone go through what I went through, Rowan. I lost so much because I was Seen."

"Miss Post."

"Fuck's sake."

The groaned words made all three of us Demons stop short. Whitaker reeled upwards, groggy and gray. "We're going to be so late, and I really don't feel like dealing with the fallout, so if we can just get this going?" His head lolled to one side, and he peered at Paulson. "I'm going to assume you have some sort of backup plan?"

Paulson looked nonplussed for all of a second. "Kill you."

"That was the primary plan. I meant what if that doesn't work?"

Lucille Post piped up. "I suggested they file an injunction against Rowan with the tribunal, but he said it'd take too long."

"Ah, an injunction. Now you're speaking my language." He made it to his feet, swaying mightily. It took all my willpower not to go to his side and prop him up.

Wait, why not?

Well. It'd make him look weak.

Uh, duh? Have you not been paying attention? He is *kind of weak right now...*

Why is my inner voice arguing with itself?

Low blood sugar, I think.

Shut up and I'll break into my emergency Twizzler stash when we get out of here.

I slipped under Whitaker's right arm and slid my hand behind his back. He stiffened in surprise, but relaxed against me soon enough, letting me take some of his weight so he didn't have to sway and lurch anymore.

"Filing an injunction takes too long, but murder is aces?" he asked. "That can only mean one thing. You're fairly certain the tribunal wouldn't move to stop Rowan. Why? Is it because what he's doing, what *we* are doing, isn't in the wrong?"

Paulson smoked ever so slightly around the edges. "All three Demons on the bench are friends of his father," Paulson snapped. "They're too blinded by their devotion to a dead Demon to see what havoc his son is wreaking!"

"Oh my God," Whitaker muttered. "I thought *you* were dramatic. Christ, is this a Demon thing, or do I just have bad luck?"

Paulson roared, punching into motion towards us. He swiped at me, grabbing for my throat. I shouted and jerked back, Whitaker tumbling with me, but the grab never came.

"You *bitch*!"

Lucille Post stood, her arms around Paulson in a bear hug, inside the circle that had entrapped me. She was crying softly as Paulson struggled against her apparently strong grasp. "Oh, my gods," I muttered. "Miss Post..."

"I'm...well. I'm not sorry for the way I feel," she said, jerking her chin defiantly. "But I am sorry I went along with him this far. I...I hate Witches—no offense, Mr. Frost—but I can't bring myself to kill one. I just can't!"

Paulson tore into her with a string of obscene imprecations, making her cry harder.

"Where's Lowery?" Whitaker demanded, seemingly oblivious to the abuse. "Where are they right now?"

"Outside. Waiting," she cried. "There's three Council members on the way."

Whitaker groaned. "Great. Well. This has been...awful." He nudged my side. "C'mon. Let's get the hell out of here before the three horsemen of the bureaucracy show up."

"Wait! You don't want to..." I trailed off, waving a hand at the Demons in the circle. "I mean, they tried to kill us, Whitaker!"

"And my mother will succeed in killing us if we're so much as two minutes late for the Solstice, Rowan. Between Demon supremacists and my mother, I'm more afraid of her than I am of them."

He was lying. Not about his mother killing us—I was pretty sure she'd be happy to off us, at least me, if we fucked up her Solstice. But he was afraid. He was scared down to his bones. I could feel it wafting off him in great waves.

I hesitated, though. I wanted to...I wanted to hurt Paulson, really hurt him. I wanted to tear them all apart for harming Whitaker, and that knowledge startled me. It was deeper than wanting to defend someone who I cared about. It was poking at a layer of feeling I wasn't anywhere near ready to face, the one where I wanted to break the world apart for Whitaker if it meant he was safe.

Goddamn, I really needed to do something about that low blood sugar.

I shook those thoughts out of the way and lied to myself that I'd look at them later. Leaving the screaming and crying behind, we limp-slid out into the foyer. It was empty, and outside, the world was twilight, casting long purple shadows through the sidelights and making the ugly yellow bench look even worse than before. "Are you sure—"

Whitaker nodded. "Honestly, this isn't my first attempted murder. The Fae are pretty stabby if you get them riled up."

He was trying to brush this off, make it less-than, and I knew that tactic well. I was a PhD in that tactic. "Okay. Okay, let's go. Lowery is still lurking, though."

Whitaker nodded. "We'll make a break for it."

"Sure, Usain, you'll just zip right out of there."

"Can you do a portal thingy?"

"Not into the car, no."

"Seriously?"

"Not unless you want me to fuck up and get us stuck halfway through the engine compartment." Portals were easy enough if you had the space, but cars...cars were tricky. There were fiddly bits that'd get damaged, electrics that would short out, and no one wanted to end up standing in their transmission. Ellery could move Between and get to a car just fine, but he was also extremely nitpicky and had practiced over a thousand times so he could get shotgun on road trips when we were kids.

Whitaker made an annoyed sound but nodded. "Okay then. We'll just...be careful."

We were plenty careful all the way to the front porch. Lowery was halfway down the drive, staring out towards the road. We had seconds before they saw us, I knew. Just long enough for me to think maybe getting stuck in the oil pan wasn't so bad if it meant getting out of harm's way.

A loud, sharp chittering erupted. Lowery jerked and turned. They weren't looking at us, though, but up in a half-dead oak tree. The sound came again, this time followed by a barrage of what looked like pine cones.

Whitaker chuckled breathlessly. "Come on. They're laying suppressing fire for us. Let's go." We hurried as best we could to the car, but he froze just beside the passenger side door. "Shit. Can you climb trees?"

"Uh, why?"

He looked up at the heavy-limbed oak nearest us. "I kind of left something in the squirrel's safekeeping earlier..."

CHAPTER TEN

Jingle bells, Rowan smells

WHITAKER

"You smell like a pine tree had sex with a muskrat, then something bad happened."

"Why is the pine tree topping? Wouldn't the muskrat be the dominant partner in that scenario?"

"Who said there's any sort of power exchange dynamic going on? Why can't the sentient pine tree and the muskrat have sex and not worry about who is the top and who is the bottom? Maybe they're both vers."

"Whitaker, drink your milkshake, or so help me gods, I am going to pour it down your throat."

I took a small sip of the butterscotch shake Rowan had insisted I needed from Sonic. It was barely eight p.m., and already the night felt late. My entire body ached in ways I'd never known possible, and my head was swimming from exhaustion, hunger, and pure old anxiety. "This is too sweet."

"It's ice cream, milk, and a hefty dose of artificial flavorings and added sugar. It's supposed to be too sweet. If you wanted a savory milkshake, you'd have to go in the summer when they do the weird flavor like chocolate jalapeno or bacon or something."

I took another tiny sip. "Bacon? Jalapeno? The south is so weird."

He chuckled wearily, taking the next entrance to the freeway. After several minutes of quiet, he asked, "Wait, how do you know what it smells like when a muskrat and pine tree bang?"

I shrugged. "I'm guessing. Between the pine sap and the squirrel shit and your own sweat...you're not exactly doing it for me right now."

Rowan narrowed his eyes but didn't look away from the road. There wasn't a lot of traffic, but freezing rain had been falling off and on since the early afternoon, and the last thing we needed was even more delays. We were already almost a day behind. I had three dozen calls from Egon and one single text from Mother demanding to know why I was insisting on causing her to die of shame.

I'd yet to return any of them.

Rowan had a few messages from Chloe, mostly shop stuff, and he'd turned his phone off and thrown it in the glove box. Not, as I first thought, for safety while driving but rather because, in his words, "If I talk to her now, she'll cry, and if she cries, Alastor and Ellery will give me shit, and I've got too much to deal with right now without adding that to my laundry list of shit to do."

Good enough for me.

"Aren't you curious at all?" he asked finally. "Don't you want to find out what the Council did? What's going on with Paulson and Lucille Post?"

"I'm more concerned with the fact two Demons are in the wind, and they were involved in this plot."

"Ugh. You know, before we got involved, I was happy running the shop, minding my own business." He ignored my snort. "I was happy enough going to the meetings and simply...being."

"We're involved?" I asked quietly.

"Um. Well." He drummed his fingers on the steering wheel, pretending to desperately need to switch lanes for a mile or so, then switch back as we drove in an odd sort of quiet. "I suppose we must be."

"Hmm." Rowan did dart a glance at me then. I took a slow sip of my milkshake—which was delicious, but I wasn't going to tell him that yet—and stared at his profile. Finally, he made a frustrated noise, and I laughed. "We haven't talked about it, but...well, I guess it's not a secret I'm attracted to you."

He snorted. "I am pretty easy on the eyes."

"Ass."

"It is pretty spectacular. All that squatting to unpack shipments at the shop."

"It's not just how nice you are to look at, jerkface. I find you very appealing on many levels."

Rowan made an odd noise. "So appealing, much sexy," he muttered, barely managing not to laugh. "You really know how to rustle a fella's jimmies there, Whit."

"Ugh, don't call me Whit. My sister calls me Whit."

"Tell me again how appealing I am. It really gets my motor running." Lowering his voice and adopting a truly awful accent meant to mimic my own cadences, he added, "Oh, Rowan, you're so appealing. I find your eyes to be such a serviceable brown color. And your lips are just made for covering your teeth. I want you to put your erect penis in my anal sphincter and thrust rhythmically until we achieve mutual satisfaction."

I flicked some of the milkshake off my straw at him. "Ew."

"Was that not appealing?" he teased.

"No, that was gross. Now my penis is sad and will never be happy again because you killed all of my boners for you forever."

"Aw, now *my* penis is sad." He pulled a ridiculously pathetic face and sniffled. "It might need mouth to mouth later."

"Mouth to mouth doesn't do anything for sadness." I paused. "And another ew for the mental image of your penis having a mouth."

He shuddered. "Okay, yeah, I took that one too far. Sorry." We drove in quiet again, both of us trying to stifle cracking yawns. I finished my milkshake and had to admit having something in my stomach made me feel better, even if it was a pint of ice cream, milk, and brown syrup.

"Hey," Rowan said quietly as we neared some mid-sized town, glaring bright on the side of the freeway. "We're gonna need to talk about this shit."

I nodded. "Yeah." I bent my straw back and forth until it creaked and cracked, then fidgeted with the cup lid until Rowan took the empty container from me and shoved it between his knees.

"Better now than later," he said softly. "I'll go first?" When I nodded, he blew out a breath and drummed those long fingers of his again. "The Demons who are anti-Revelation...I used to think that maybe if we just got Witches to agree on the truth of the matter, that their powers came from Demons originally, that the Fae may have shown them the Wellspring, but our magic was what *made* Witches able to use the Wellspring...well. I thought maybe that would be the path towards unity, you know?"

"Make Witches unlearn everything they've believed for generations?" I asked. "I'm not saying you're wrong, mind, but just...that's a lot to expect of an entire group of people in one fell swoop."

He made a sour face. "I know you're not the only Witch who isn't hidebound with the old ideas. There's others..."

"And there's Demons who support what you're doing, but where are they now? Hiding in the trunk? Or are they going to meet us at my family home for the Solstice day after tomorrow?" It wasn't fair, I knew, but the words came anyway. "Besides Ellery and probably Alastor, what other living Demon do you know who wants to be part of this Revelation? Every one I've met except for you and your brothers have been marked either by apathy or outright refusal."

"There are others," he said. "They're afraid."

At his soft gasp, I sighed. "I can't pretend I don't know that," I murmured. "What are they afraid of?"

"You heard Lucille Post earlier. Afraid of retribution. Demons like Paulson...well, that think like him. They can make life exceedingly difficult for Demons who think like I do but don't have the family name to shield them. Dozens of smaller clans in our community lack the resources or social capital to make any waves and are constantly pushed back by the older names. If I wasn't a Hebert, I'd..."

The milkshake was sitting heavily now. "You'd what? What would have happened to you if your family wasn't an old name, Rowan?"

He blew out a rough breath. "Nothing."

"Rowan..."

"I mean it. Nothing. I'd have been ignored. Worst case? Bullied and maybe beaten. No powerful family means I wouldn't be worth making an example of. And...and I never would have made it as far as I have. Demonborn would never have made it this far."

I nodded. "You're carrying them all on your back."

"No. No, I'm not, Heliotrope got things going, at least this time. And your grandmother helped. Oh, my gods, she helped. If it hadn't been for her reaching out to Heliotrope ages ago..." He shook his head again. "Well."

"Well."

WE STOPPED FOR THE night, or what was left of it, in a small town across the border into Tennessee. The hotel was surprisingly large and seemed made for conventions and business meetings, boasting six different conference rooms on the first floor and two separate business lounges. We were given a double room smelling faintly of cigarettes and industrial cleaner, all the decor done in shades of taupe and mauve. "It's like the mid-90s came here to die," Rowan murmured, dropping his bags at the foot of the bed nearest the door. "You want to shower first or should I?"

I shrugged but shuffled to the bathroom anyway. We passed one another silently, getting ready for bed. I showered, he brushed his teeth, and then it was time to switch. By the time we settled into our respective beds, the tension was unwieldy. "What," I said over the hum of the room's heater, "the fuck was all of that anyway?"

"The way Alastor figures, the bits of magic they were taking from you were meant to help frame me." Rowan rolled onto his side and faced me. He looked haggard, older than his thirty years by a wide margin. "We were just lucky that little fetch of yours was kindly disposed towards me and did as I asked."

I huffed a laugh. "That's because that fetch is me, in essence. It's not just something I created."

"That's so weird," he muttered.

I rolled to face him more fully. "They delayed us by a day, but we should still make it in time. I'll bite the bullet and call Egon in the morning."

"Don't you think you should get in touch with him tonight?"

Rowan was probably right, but the very idea of having to talk to Egon at all, or rather being talked at by him, made my already throbbing headache threaten to explode into an avalanche of pain. "It will keep. The Council members who were summoned will tell him I'm fine. I'd rather wait and talk to him when I have at least a few hours of sleep."

Rowan nodded, his eyes already heavy. "I'm sorry for today," he said quietly, voice thick. "I feel like it's my fault."

"No." My whisper was fierce. I wanted to reach out and touch his face, his hair, feel his breath on my fingers and assure him—or maybe assure myself—he was okay, he was alive, and he understood what I was saying even if my words were inadequate. "No, it's not your fault at all. It's theirs for being fucking obsessed with a way of life that no longer exists. It's their fault for deciding what they did was the right course of action instead of at least three other paths I can think of off the top of my head, and that's just with my own scant familiarity with Demon cultures."

When he spoke again, his voice was slurred with sleep. "Hey, Whitaker? Just so you know...you're appealing, too."

WE OVERSLEPT, WHICH shouldn't have surprised me at all, but I couldn't help feeling annoyed and more than a little guilty, especially after I saw the good morning text from my mother, asking if I was dead and if so would I be so good as to make an appearance for the medium she'd hired as she'd paid a nice little sum, and she'd like to get her money's worth. Rowan wasn't in the room when I rolled out of bed at nine, but he hadn't gone far. The coffee pot was still dripping what passed for coffee at the hotel, and the bathroom was still emitting a gentle waft of generic soap-scented steam with an undercurrent of pine and squirrel.

The hotel room door swung open as I sat bleary-eyed and wondering if I should suggest bathing in tomato juice to get rid of the squirrel funk. Rowan clutched a paper bag in his teeth and the morning paper under one arm, along with a plastic grocery sack in the other hand. He grinned around the paper bag and dropped it on the bed with an exaggerated *puh* sound. "Kolaches. There's a shop across the street. And lunch." He rattled the plastic sack. "Grabbed some sandwiches and chips and drinks from the grocery down the block."

I glanced at the still-steamy bathroom again. "You're fast."

"Demons are great at power-walking. True story." With a wink, he tore into his kolache while grabbing one of the Styrofoam room cups. "Take a look at page six," he said around a mouthful of bread and sausage.

I tugged the paper closer and flipped to page six. "Local city councilman indicted in money-laundering scheme."

"Down a story." He added an obscene amount of sugar to his coffee. "Tell me what you think."

"I think you're going to be able to see sound if you have any more sugar today," I said but glanced down at the next article obligingly. "Oh. Oh, that's not great, is it?" A grim little black-and-white image of a few people with protest signs with sayings like *Humans First, Last, and Always* and *Devil Be Gone* were standing in front of a storefront, looking determined and very organized.

"Humans First," Rowan said, swallowing his last mouthful of breakfast. "Apparently, there's a national movement gaining some small bit of traction, claiming humans are being subjugated beneath the will of supernatural beings. Of course," he added, tapping one of the lines about halfway through the article, "they don't say it as politely."

I scanned the vitriol, a niggle of unease vying for attention with my hunger. "If this is real, how did they find out? We've been beyond careful. You don't live for centuries hidden in plain sight without learning to...well, hide in plain sight!"

Rowan shrugged. "I have some suspicions but nothing solid. I did send Alastor a link to the online version of the article, though. He likes to keep track of any time Demons are mentioned in the media, just to make sure it's bullshit and nothing we need to worry about."

"Does that happen often?" I tried to think back on the last time anyone had mentioned anything about real, honest-to-gods Witches in the media. I was drawing a blank.

Rowan grinned, baring his teeth like some feral thing. "This is the first time it's been legit," he said. "Ever."

"Shit."

"Pretty much. Now. Eat up, drink up, and let's get our asses in gear. Call your minder before he decides to try and find me," he added, heading for his bags. "He doesn't find me as appealing as you do."

"THE COUNCIL WAS QUITE disturbed by these allegations, Whitaker," Egon said in a sharp, dry tone. "We sent three of the security team to this location last night, certain that Demonspawn—"

"Demonborn," I corrected, already exhausted. "They prefer Demonborn or just Demon. And it was a false alarm."

He sniffed. "This time. What else could that Demon possibly want with you, Whitaker, if not your influence in the Council? You're hardly his type."

"How would you know what his type is?" I looked at Rowan sitting in the car, this time in the passenger seat, bopping his head to the radio as he fiddled with his own phone. Before we left the hotel, he'd fired off an angry text or six to Chloe and ordered her to close the shop unless Ellery was there to help, since she couldn't keep her mouth shut around customers.

"Please," Egon sneered. "You think for one moment he hasn't had every possible security scan and background check run on him since the moment he appeared on our radar?" He made a tutting sound and said in a pitying tone, "You're hardly the first powerful man he's cozied up to, Whitaker."

Jealousy plucked at something in my chest, but I swallowed it down, refusing to be baited. At least not yet. "I thought you said I wasn't his type." While Egon sputtered, I pressed on. "We'll be there with the bells—yes, they're safe—in time for the Solstice. Unless something remarkable happens, you don't need to contact me before then."

I hung up and waited for nearly two full minutes before letting out a sigh of relief. I'd fully expected him to call me right back, ready to fight, but the longer the phone went without vibrating in my hand, the better I felt.

I made my way back to the car, pausing before I opened the door. Rowan was smiling at something on his phone, his dimples deep and fucking adorable. He laughed, tossing his head back, and I thought of how he had looked in the bathroom at the Equinox, on his bed in that tiny apartment over the shop. I wanted to see him look like that again, and soon.

It wasn't merely the sex I wanted with him, either. I wanted to unravel all of those knots he'd bound himself in, untangle him until he felt free enough to let me see him without the prickly shield all the time.

He looked up and saw me, his grin wide as he waved his phone at me. *Look at this*, he mouthed.

I slid into the driver's seat and leaned across as he held his phone up. Whatever the meme was, I didn't see it, instead pulling him into a kiss across the center console.

"Oh, hello," he murmured against my lips. "What's that for? This is new for us."

"Do you mind?" I asked, still close enough our lips brushed with our words. I felt his breath on my cheek and shivered at how it tickled along my ear. "I can stop."

"Mmm. I rather like it," he admitted. He shifted a bit and winced. "Sorry, that's not you. It's the star in my pocket."

"I thought you were just happy to see me," I teased, earning an eye roll and a gentle shove. "We good to go?"

He nodded. "I'm ready if you are."

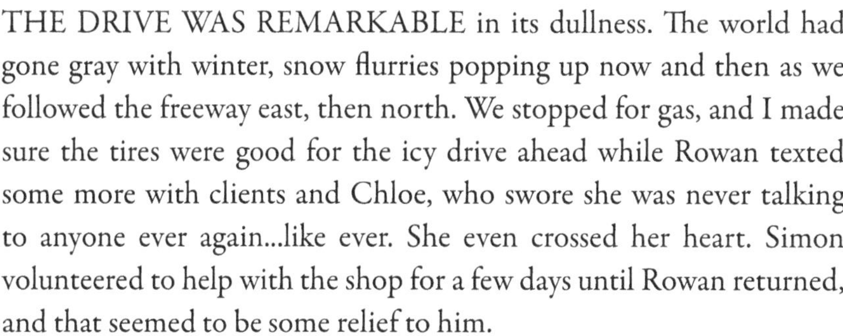

THE DRIVE WAS REMARKABLE in its dullness. The world had gone gray with winter, snow flurries popping up now and then as we followed the freeway east, then north. We stopped for gas, and I made sure the tires were good for the icy drive ahead while Rowan texted some more with clients and Chloe, who swore she was never talking to anyone ever again...like ever. She even crossed her heart. Simon volunteered to help with the shop for a few days until Rowan returned, and that seemed to be some relief to him.

I ducked into the men's room inside the service station to wash my hands, thinking maybe I'd grab a coffee on my way back to the car and wondering if Rowan maybe wanted another, since he seemed to run almost exclusively on carbs and caffeine.

"You need to know," a voice said quietly from behind me.

"Uh, occupied," I said, turning to face Demaris. Part of me was not surprised in the slightest. He and his cohort had vanished on us, and I'd doubted they'd go meekly into retirement just because Paulson and Lucille Post were...well, probably arrested by the Council at this point.

"You need to know," he repeated, his gaze unfocused, "that the Demonborn will not be put under your heel. We will not become the monsters under the bed, the scapegoats for your failures, your bad examples." He brought one hand up and, before I could even shout, brought it down swiftly. I flinched back from a flow that never came. Demaris just...vanished. There was no portal, no special effects. He was simply gone.

Shaken and suddenly very wide awake, I hurried back to the car. Rowan was sitting bolt upright, eyes wide. "Demaris," I began. He nodded.

"His little friend was here, too. I saw him waiting, just there." He pointed to the cage where the propane tanks were stored for sale. "We need to go."

While I got us back onto the freeway, Rowan called Alastor. He relayed the encounter to his brother and then went quiet, muttering the occasional agreement or disbelief to whatever Alastor was telling him. Finally, he groaned, said goodbye, and tossed his phone into the cupholder. "Bad news or worse news?"

"Oh, surprise me," I sighed, aiming the car northwards.

"Alastor figures that the little bits of magic they pulled from you made them able to find out where we are. Stolen magic wants to return to its source and will do anything to get there. Downside of that means it's easy to follow if you know what you're doing, and these asshats definitely knew what they were doing. Slightly good news? They were likely able only to do it once. Stolen magic isn't shelf-stable. It goes off fast."

For a mile or so, we were both quiet while the implications of what else they could do or could have done with stolen magic settled over us. Some Witches had made studies of magic, more than just grimoires and spells and such. Deep dives into the matter of it, the philosophy and physics. I wondered if there was any chance I could get a look at some of those studies.

If these Demons could steal from me—and I'm not boasting when I say I'm a fairly strong Witch from an old, deep-rooted family—what could they do with a Witch who wasn't able to protect themselves at all? With a Fae who had been weakened by iron or... I shook myself mentally. That was something I'd need to present to the Council, something we'd need to research if this was going to be a threat.

"What's the worse news?"

"Apparently, the Council's decided I'm up to some shit, and they've put a price on my head. So to speak." He chuckled weakly. "At least I hope that's a metaphor." He glanced at me. "That is a metaphor with them, isn't it?"

I smiled tightly. "Sure, Rowan. Sure."

"Whitaker..."

"When we stop for the night, I'll call Egon again." I sighed. I half suspected Egon was behind that anyway, a reminder he had the power in this situation and if I didn't toe the line for him and get the bells back on time, he could not only make my life Hell—he'd make Rowan's life even worse. "He'll be able to tell us what the Council wants from you exactly."

"According to Alastor, when they contacted him today looking for me, they would like to know where I put the silver bells and..." he paused, his expression pinched and angry. "And why I revealed the existence of Demons to humans."

"What?"

Rowan sighed, pinching the bridge of his nose. "Winter Solstice has always been my least favorite holiday," he muttered. "When bad shit happens, it's always at the Solstice. Nothing bad ever happens at the Autumnal Equinox. That's why I like it. I can have my pumpkin spice coffee, burn my apple cinnamon candles, and nobody does anything crazy."

He lifted his face and tipped it up towards the ceiling. "Alastor is on it, as much as he can be, trying to get to the bottom of the Humans First rumors. He thinks he's found a connection to Paulson with those and said I shouldn't worry too much about them, but for fuck's sake! The Council thinks I'm involved and told these yahoos Demons are not only real, but proved it by demonstrating a sigil portal to them!"

"Would a Demon have done that? I mean...like if one of you married a human, could they show their partner?"

"Darling, I love you. Let me show you my interdimensional gateway. Yes, it's large, but it's not the size that matters. It's how you use it." He slid down in the seat, unable to keep still as we sped through the thickening snowfall towards whatever was waiting for us with the Council, with home. "It's...not encouraged," he finally admitted. "Simon knows about Ellery, obviously, and therefore the rest of us, but Simon isn't a typical human."

Ellery's boyfriend Simon had been raised as a changeling by the Fae until he was eighteen. Then he was excommunicated from the only life he'd known, until an incident earlier in the year had brought him back into contact with Fae. He now had an honorary position as Human-Super liaison for the Council. That position, of course, was dependent on whenever we got our shit together and got things rolling.

"Simon's definitely a special case, no matter what supernatural communities are involved," I agreed. "But Joe Blow marries Debbie Demon, for example. Can Debbie show Joe what she is?"

Rowan made a face. "I mean...yeah? It's up to the Demon, but," he said thoughtfully, "while it's not encouraged, we're also discouraged from hiding our nature. It's a very tangled-up situation and one of the main reasons Demons don't generally partner long-term with humans. But this thing? The accusations being thrown at me?" He shook his head. "That's not the same as me showing a human partner that neat trick I can do with the fire or drawing a healing sigil for a sick friend. This is malicious. It's endangering." He shook his head again. "Alastor is on it, and he's terrifying when he wants to be. He said he's getting the Council off my back, but..." He sighed and closed his eyes. "Fuck." He was quiet for so long, I thought he'd fallen asleep. After several more miles, he said, "Next rest stop, let's switch."

I nodded, my own thoughts churning along with my nerves.

CHAPTER ELEVEN

G*ods bless us, every one. Except that guy. Fuck that guy.*

ROWAN

"Shit."

"We're gonna have to stop for the night."

"But we're so close," Whitaker sighed. "Okay, pull in at the next hotel you see."

I shot him a look. "It's near whiteout conditions! I can't see anything!"

Whitaker leaned forward, squinting out the windshield. "You know, if you were able to make it snow back in Houston..."

"That was different. Making it snow isn't the same as making it stop snowing. It's like trying to shove biscuits back into the can, making it stop."

"Biscuits don't come in cans..."

"You poor, naive summer child." A flash of orange and green off to my right gave me a spark of hope. "Okay, I don't care what that neon belongs to. We're stopping there for the night." *Please be a hotel, please be a hotel...* "Jackpot!" I crowed, turning the car carefully into what I hoped was the driveway and not a ditch.

"Seriously? The Horse U Rode Inn?"

"Beggars, choosers, yada yada yada." I pulled under the portico and left the engine running for Whitaker while jogging into the tiny, warm lobby. Whitaker scowled at me from the passenger window like a very handsome yet annoyed dog. Maybe I'd bring him a treat if he stayed in the car and behaved.

"Let me guess...two rooms?"

I grinned at the young woman behind the desk. "One, actually."

"Ooooooh, I get it," she giggled. She leaned past me to look at Whitaker. "He's cute."

"I find him appealing," I agreed solemnly. Her brow quirked, but she shrugged it off and rang up my card for a queen bed on the first floor, handed me a brochure for Winter Fun Day in Willard, New York, and told me to give the heater a good smack if it didn't turn on when I pressed the switch. When I got back to the car, Whitaker was still scowling. "Nothing but the best for us, babe," I said, tossing him the brochure and room key.

"I'm babe now?" he asked, his cheeks a bit pinker than they'd been a moment before. "That's new."

I weighed several replies, but none of them felt right. They were too crass, too flippant, too...something. Instead, I just hummed, drove us around the side of the building, and parked right outside our room for the night. We grabbed our things and made a dash for the door, shivering and stomping as we wiggled our way inside, slamming the door behind us. I smacked the heater around as we shed our outer layers.

Whitaker's teeth were chattering hard, so I pulled him close to me and let a tiny bit of Demon fire glow through me, warming us both in no time. "I'm very handy to have around in cold weather," I informed him. "Summers are a bitch, though."

He smiled down at me and didn't let go when I tried to step back. "From what I remember, summers weren't that bad."

"You only had me for a few hours in summer," I reminded him, the words coming out far less teasing than I intended. Almost sad.

Frowning, Whitaker smoothed his thumb along my jaw. "I'd like to try for longer this summer."

Oh. *Oh.* He was already leaning towards me when I tilted my chin up to catch him in a kiss. It was slow at first, warm from the heat I'd radiated, sliding into something deeper and harder. He walked me back until my knees hit the bed, stilling the kiss as we broke for breath. "It's okay," I said as his hands settled on my hips. "I mean, if you want to."

He nodded, hard. "I really do. It's been on my mind pretty much constantly since...well. Since the bathroom at the Equinox."

There were a million other things we needed to worry about—Paulson, the Humans First group, the damned bells, the one missing stranger's bell...but all of it was a blur and distant as his hands slipped under my shirt and I curled my fingers into the hair at the nape of his neck. His rough stubble was painful and delicious at once as his kisses moved to my jaw, then my throat. I whined, shifting from foot to foot, trying to make my cock feel less constricted in the confines of my jeans. Whitaker had some pity on me and reached for the button and zipper, giving me some breathing room as he freed my erection.

"Not too fast," I murmured when he dipped his fingers into my briefs. "We have some time."

Whitaker grinned against me. "It never feels like we do, does it? Quick handjobs in the bathroom, a fast fuck on your bed..."

"Well, how about this," I murmured, pulling away to crawl to the middle of the bed. "When this is all said and done, we'll turn off our phones, lock the doors, and go at it for like...a day and a half."

"That's a very specific amount of time," he said, crawling after me.

"Two days is too long, one day isn't long enough. Day and a half is factoring in naps, food breaks, and the occasional rehydration break."

"Smart man." He pushed me onto my back. "I love smart men."

"Aren't I lucky," I crooned, unable to stop myself from giggling as his bristles tickled my belly. He nipped me just below my navel, darting his tongue out to lave the wet tip of my cock, peeking from beneath the waistband of my briefs. I wiggled as he tugged my jeans down, arching into his hands. He had my clothes off in no time and his own soon after.

We couldn't stop touching one another, hands and mouths constantly moving over skin, our hard lengths brushing against one another as we rolled on the bed, each trying to make the other moan louder, longer than the other. Whitaker won that tussle when he managed to get me on my stomach and tugged my hips, so I was face-down on the mattress. "What," I started to say, only for the word to die off in a keening moan as his tongue dragged down the cleft of my ass, the stiffened tip brushing over the furl of my hole.

Gasping, I arched back, shoving myself against him. He laughed and licked me again, then again, parting my cheeks to make a meal of me as he lapped and laved. I was lost to the sensations, unable to quiet the babble pouring from my mouth under his intense ministrations.

Lovers in the past did this for me, but never with Whitaker's enthusiasm and attention. He found the spots making me moan the loudest, the technique making my entire body melt. I was nearly incoherent by the time he pressed one, then two fingers into my softened hole, his tongue still working me as he thrust slowly in and out. Before long, my orgasm rushed down my spine, pooling low in my belly. My entire body bowed and went tight as Whitaker wrapped his fingers around my leaking cock, giving me one, two strokes before I sobbed out my release.

He gently eased me onto my back, his own cock angry and purple-tipped. "Come on me," I whispered. "Mark me. Please, Whitaker. Mark me, make me yours." It was a lot, saying that, but it was what I wanted—what I hoped he wanted, too.

We'd been dancing around one another for over a year now, this connection between us something beyond physical. We clicked, the two of us, our rough edges smoothing one another out. I wanted to be his; I wanted him to be mine. I wanted to say that to him, tell him all of it, but I bit down on the words. During sex wasn't the time, not if I wanted him to believe me.

His loud gasp broke my train of thought. He stroked his cock fast, his hand a blur over the turgid length of it, and with a loud, low grunt, he bowed over me and came, striping my stomach and chest and chin with ribbons of cum. Shaking, he lowered himself to the bed next to me and pulled me close, neither of us caring about the mess we'd made and were making worse.

"In the morning," he said quietly after I don't know how long, "we need to head out early if we can."

I nodded. "But we're here for tonight. We're safe in here, warm..." I yawned. "You're warm."

I could hear the smile in his voice. "Thanks to you."

"Warm and sticky. My cinnamon bun."

"Ew."

"Ew," I agreed and snuggled in close. Tomorrow, we'd be at his family home. It was the Solstice. We still didn't have the final bell, and I didn't know what that meant for us, for the Witches, for any of it, but for the moment, we had our bubble. We could hold on to one another without anyone looming over us, making demands of us. We could just be.

I HAD NEVER EXPERIENCED Solstice with Witches before.

I knew their observations were different than Demonborns', but I hadn't realized how much. It wasn't the decorations—the Frosts leaned heavily in the Martha Stewart Holiday Home Collection direction, with a bit of old world weird thrown in for good measure. It wasn't even the way the magic practically seeped into my pores as soon as we stepped onto the property.

It was the sheer intensity of it, the feeling of ancient power wrapped with vitality and an undercurrent of death.

When Demons held our celebrations, they were far more...arcane, I suppose is the best word for it.

There were a lot of rocks and astronomy involved. We're pretty big into astronomy.

The fact the Witches solstice celebration was being held concurrently with the Council meeting added an extra layer of nerve-wracking energy for me.

"Breathe," Whitaker muttered, leading me to the sweeping front steps of the Frost home. "I promise no one here will turn you into a newt."

"Witch humor, nice."

"No, it's true. Turning people into newts was outlawed in 1802. Now we can only do certain species of toads, field mice, and the occasional large goat."

"Occasional goat?"

"Like an occasional table," he said with a small grin. "But much harder to integrate into the décor."

We laughed, passing a cluster of witches on the steps. I braced for glares or even curses—literal or figurative—but they just regarded both of us curiously and resumed their conversation before we were even past them.

"Whitaker!"

"Brace yourself," he whispered as we mounted the porch steps. "She's in attack mode."

"From the little bit I know of her, isn't that permanent?"

He snorted. "I'd be mad, but you're not wrong. Mother," he said, changing tones. "You remember Rowan Hebert."

She looked at his hand, rested on my forearm, at how close we were standing. "I remember the Heberts." Smile like ice, she turned on her three-inch heels and led us into the house. We wound our way through corridors Whitaker knew well until we finally fetched up in a small, dark study. "Egon's wrapping up a meeting with one of the Sidhe council in preparation for tomorrow's festivities," she said with icicles in her voice. "If you'll excuse me, I have some matters to attend to with the kitchen staff, but I'll be back for this...meeting." Pausing in the doorway, she eyed Whitaker. "Do you have them?"

We exchanged glances. "I have the box that was sent to Heliotrope's store, yes."

Mrs. Frost cocked her head to one side. "What aren't you saying?" She sniffed, leaning in close. "You've been spending too much time with a Demon, to start talking like them."

Whitaker shook his head. "We'll discuss it at the meeting."

I sank back in my chair and closed my eyes, fingers tight on that plastic star, my focus fidget over the past week. We'd looked for the thirteenth bell, even getting Lydia to exert her Charm on the shipping company guys again, but there had been nothing, not a single trace. Even my Demon magic had failed. We'd turned in circles, directed again to wherever we were standing each time I tried.

"We'll make it work somehow," he murmured as soon as his mother shut the door. "There has to be some sort of failsafe built into the process."

I nodded, knowing it was not going to go well at all. After a few tense minutes, the door swung open, and the old man I remembered from the Summer Solstice meeting was there. Egon St. Ives. "Gentlemen," he cried as if we were long-lost friends. "Finally! Cutting it a bit fine, hm? Tomorrow's the Solstice." His gaze fell on the box, a slow smile curving his thin lips. "And this is it, hm?"

Whitaker pushed the box forward. "We have some questions. Like why do these bells seem to be warded against Demonborn?"

"I suppose because they're forbidden to touch them. No offense," Egon added, giving me one of those smirks saying otherwise. "The curse goes back hundreds of years. Demonborn are not like us. They cannot mingle with us, cannot share in our magics."

"Why not?" I asked. "Without the Demons who fell in love with humans eons ago and wanted to share their knowledge, you wouldn't have a single drop of magic in your body. But you know that, don't you?"

Egon sniffed so hard I was surprised he didn't pull something. "That Faerie tale is lovely, I'm sure, but it has as much truth to it as," he waved one hand airily, "oh, one of those ridiculous cartoon movies. The one with the ogre."

"Did he just compare my ancestors to Shrek?" I asked Whitaker. "Seriously?"

"Where's the thirteenth one?" Egon had been digging through the box while I spoke to Whit and was obviously, glaringly, displeased. "We need all thirteen. It was sent to you. Where did you put it?" He bent low to get in my face, but Whitaker was faster, putting himself between Egon and me in a heartbeat. "Move, Whitaker!"

He pushed Whit aside with a flick of his wrist, sending Whit sprawling across the rug. I jumped to my feet, stepping between Egon and Whitaker, bringing my hands up to push Egon away with a tiny bit of Demonborn magic. Before I could summon so much as a mild shove, Egon lifted me with a hand to my throat. His fingers dug in against my carotids, his palm pushing hard on my windpipe. Panic slammed through me, taking over and shutting down magic as I struggled.

Part of me knew I could be free of Egon's grasp in a few simple thoughts. A push of magic to burn his hand, buckle his bones, send his own fear response through the roof with merely a twist of my fingers and push of my will. But panic won.

He shook me like a ragdoll, my breath thick in my lungs and burning hot.

Whitaker pushed to his hands and knees, but Egon was fast. He hissed a word, not even bothering to glance at Whitaker, and sent him sprawling back again, buffeting against the stone hearth.

My struggling wriggled Egon's grasp just loose enough for a sip of air to escape. "No," I hissed, the sound burning my throat. I kicked Egon's knee. I don't know if I surprised him or hurt him, just that he slackened his grip enough for me to fall back, landing on my ass. I pushed away, shoving myself to my feet before he could grab for me again.

"You seek to defile the council," he snarled, turning to limp towards me and corner me. "I cannot let that happen. Lucinda was soft, too soft, and saw nothing wrong with it. She wanted this division to end, always said we'd be stronger for it, but she was ignorant. If we let Demons stand in council with us, we will be *weak*."

"You're not afraid of what we can do," I realized. "You're afraid of what we are and that it's stronger than you. We don't need the Wellspring like Witches do. We're born with an infinite supply of power."

Snarling, he lunged at me again. Whitaker rolled to his feet, shouldering him aside.

I stumbled sideways, hitting the door with my hip. The plastic star in my pocket cracked, the sharp edge drawing blood again. Something warm spread through me. Had that damn piece of plastic managed to hit a major vein?

Then the warm sensation transformed. It felt...lovely. Perfect. Like being held in my grandmother's arms when I was little, hearing her whisper to me when I couldn't sleep, wrapping up in her quilt on the sofa, listening to the evening news with her. It felt like love. Welcome. Home.

And it was so distracting Egon managed to shove me down as he twisted away from Whitaker. "I have worked too hard to become the clans' leader. Too hard, gods damn it!"

I rolled to one side, a warm spot of blood on my upper thigh from where the star jabbed me spreading, trickling down my leg.

A small and silvery bell pealed, making Egon freeze. "What," he demanded, "is that? Where are you hiding it?"

I scrambled back, letting Whitaker pull me to my feet. Egon lunged for the box on the desk, pulling the large bells out and throwing them aside. "I hear it! You have the last one!"

Whitaker was staring at me strangely, his eyes moving from my face to my hip, where the bloodstain was slowly spreading. "It's in your pocket," he said quietly. "Ro..."

I brought out the crushed plastic star—and a tiny silver bell the size of my pinky nail. It had a smear of blood, my blood, on it, ringing like someone was shaking it within an inch of its life.

Egon stared at us wild-eyed for a long, breathless moment. Then, before I could think to shield myself against him, he brought up his hands and clapped them loud and hard one time.

The fire in the hearth whooshed out, swirling into a whirlwind of flame and crashing over me. Whitaker screamed, and someone shouted for help. The fire moved over me in what was surely seconds but could have been minutes, hours, days, improbably slow and soft, not painful at all. It diminished, leaving me feeling a little too warm but not burned.

"Rowan," Whitaker cried hoarsely, lunging towards me. He grabbed the rug between us, a long and likely hideously expensive thing older than both of us put together, and dragged it toward me to smother the fire. He was shouting, but I couldn't make out his words, just the sheer terror in his voice, the sound of a man flayed raw with fear.

"It's okay," I said shakily. "Demonborn. His fire can't hurt me." I'd have to make sure Whitaker knew that didn't apply to regular fire; I would still burn. But magical fire? Fire conjured by a Witch, like Egon St. Ives? Not even a blister.

Egon was pinned face-down on the desk by Lydia, breathing hard and looking rough with a fresh bruise blooming on her face. Her hair was in wild disarray, bits of holly and ivy hanging from her curls.

Mrs. Frost stood in the doorway, stock-still and pale. "Sorry we're late," Mrs. Frost said faintly. "I... I stopped to speak with the Linton clan's matriarch. Lydia heard shouting..."

Lydia nodded. “Hey,” she panted. “Look, Whitaker! I told you taking Judo would be good for me!”

Whitaker finally spoke. "We're convening an emergency council meeting. Now."

'NOW' WAS ACTUALLY THREE hours later. Three hours, during which Egon St. Ives was locked in the wine cellar (not a cool, damp, stone room like I'd imagined, but rather a climate-controlled vault with a heavy-duty computerized lock), I was given a sparkly bandage with ponies on it for the gouge on my leg, and the thirteen bells, including the one now baptized in my blood, were gingerly gathered and taken to the ritual site for consecration and safekeeping.

"That's almost anti-climactic," I sighed. "I don't know what I was expecting. A bit more fanfare, maybe?"

Whitaker groaned tiredly. "We can do fanfare later. I want this to be over with first." He laid his arm across my shoulders and pulled me in close. "I was terrified," he admitted softly. "I didn't know what to do. I'd never seen Egon or anyone go off like that. And I was sure you were dead..."

"Nope," I teased, trying to lighten the mood and failing, "you're stuck with me a while longer."

His muttered 'good' was so soft I could pretend not to hear it if I chose. Instead, I laced my fingers with his and repeated the word. "Good."

Soon, council members tottered in. As it turned out, they kept dedicated mediums on payroll. A lanky young man with a wild mop of dark hair and a decidedly puckish expression was brought into the large study where the meeting was being held. Everyone was on their best behavior, and I wondered if the young man knew he was in a room full of Witches and one very tired Demonborn.

"Two older ladies," he said in a soft British accent. "One for you," he pointed at Whit. "And one for you." My turn. "They conspired, knowing they'd never live long enough to see the day when the stranger was welcome in with the clans, but set a plan in motion to make it happen." He smiled at us both. "And I don't know why, but they keep showing me Harry Potter," he indicated Whitaker again, "and...Ron Perlman?" *Hellboy* reference? *Thanks, Grandma.*

After that, everything descended into chaos. We managed to shuffle out to the hotel, where we stayed until very late the next day. We'd discussed it and decided, post a lot of debate, to make a very short Solstice ritual appearance. After all, my blood was on the damn bell now, and I had to take part in order to activate their Wellspring.

"Don't be nervous," Whitaker murmured, leading me up the front steps for the second time in less than twenty-four hours. Unlike the day before, with the thin edge of festivity in the air, the day of the ritual was tense.

"That's like telling me not to think of purple elephants."

"Why would you be thinking of purple elephants?"

"I wasn't until you said something!"

"I didn't say anything!"

"I'm gonna be sick." We stopped mid-step, halfway to the top (seriously, who needs this many front steps?). "Whitaker, what if I ruin everything?" I asked quietly, voicing the fear that had kept me up all night, nibbling at my nerves like a mouse. "This is the Solstice. This is *huge* for Witches. If me being here fucks everything up..."

He slid his hands up my arms and pulled me a pace closer, close enough to feel his breath feather across my cheek as he leaned in close to whisper, "I have a secret to tell you: It wouldn't be the first time the Solstice ritual got fucked up." He winked, pulling back as I uttered a startled bark of laughter. "We've been doing this for centuries. It's not uncommon for someone to fumble a word or just outright do something *wrong* during the ritual. I'll tell you a secret about Witch magic, my dear Demon. It's meant to be imperfect. It comes from here," he touched his chest," and here," his forehead. "Even if I said the wrong words, if I meant for that leaf to swoop up in the air and land on your nose, it would," He pointed at a brown, soggy leaf laying at our feet and said, "Peanut brittle." The leaf did as he'd imagined and booped my nose.

"That's disgustingly wet," I muttered.

"And you're surprisingly nervous." He booped me with the leaf again before sending it soaring out into the yard to disappear amongst the others beneath the trees. "This is what you wanted..."

"Kind of? And you know what they say about getting what you want."

"It's awesome?"

His mother had impeccable timing. Before I could counter his witty rejoinder, she opened the doors above us. "It's nearly time," she said, sounding far more subdued than she had the day before. "Rowan, please come in. As the Stranger, you have an important part to play."

Shit. "Of course."

She led us through the house, past a few knots of people drinking something sharp-smelling and herbal, past a dining room that looked as it if it were lifted from a palace, and through an orangerie where the trees were blooming white and fragrant and, unlike the gloomy day outdoors, the sun seemed to be shining beneath a blue sky visible over our heads. "Mind your step," she murmured as we exited the glass room and entered a magnificent garden.

"It's winter," Whitaker said quietly as we entered a massive pergola made from some sort of polished, pale wood with a roof of thick, green leaves, dotted with red and white berries.

"Holly and ivy," I chuckled. "I'm not entirely ignorant in the ways of the Witch."

The group already gathered was a mix of nonplussed to see a Demon in their midst, and mildly interested. In the center of the space was a smooth, bare patch of dirt the size of a small car and everyone was gathered around it, giving it a wide berth but still centering it. "Stand right here," Nanette Frost ordered, pointing to an empty spot. "Whitaker—"

"You'll be fine," he assured me, heading for a spot across the circle from me, between Nanette and an older man who had to be his father.

Nanette hurried back across to me and motioned for my hand. She pressed the small Stranger's Bell into it and closed my fingers over it none-too-gently. "The Stranger is among us," she said just a bit too loudly to be conversational. "Welcome them to our Rite."

The mood shifted dramatically. All eyes turned to me and, as one, the Witches intoned, "Hail and welcome."

"Um. Hi?"

Whitaker snorted softly.

"I mean. Thank you for welcoming me."

"We shall begin," Whitaker said. "As is tradition and law, we welcome the stranger among us at the Solstice. As Witches have since the first of us learned the Signs and Words, we have made space for the Stranger in our magic and our circles." He paused, and I was fairly certain there was definitely some awkward, guilty shuffling going on with some of the Witches around me. "In years past, we've both had Strangers in body and blood, and Stranger in thought. When we welcome them, we accept their magic, or lack of, as part of our world. And they join in the ancient chants that first opened us to our own magic. Our chimes, forged of the stars that fell when we were still in the dark, resonate with our ancient power. The bell of the stranger, made from the silver brought from deep in the earth, joins with ours to complete the resonance."

Whitaker made a short, sharp gesture in my direction. "Rowan, of the Demonborn, we welcome you to this Rite and invite you to join with us in welcoming back the Wellspring, the source of Witch magic and—" he hesitated, looking uncertain for the first time all evening.

He took a short, sharp breath and said in a rush, "The source of Witch magic and a gift from your own ancestors to ours."

A ripple of displeasure and surprise raced through the circle but no one stepped out. No one tried to stop proceedings. Whitaker was pale, his hands shaking a little as he raised them up in a benediction-like gesture. "Welcome our source of magic, our ancient wellspring, into our circle."

"Ring," Nanette hissed a moment before the rest of the bells begin to chime, twelve Witches shaking them gently. I joined in, the soft ring of the silver bell in my hand trilling like birdsong among the louder, deeper chimes of the others. The noise was almost too much at first but after just a few seconds, it settled into a sort of rolling wave of sound and I felt like I was floating. It shivered through me, no longer a sound in my ears but a vibration in my bones. After I don't know how long, the witch beside me gave me a tiny nudge and I realized the others had stopped.

"Sorry," I muttered, holding the bell down by my side.

In the center of the circle, where the bare patch had been, was a large stone I wouldn't have looked at twice if I'd been out on a hike. Barely the size of my old Fiesta, it looked unassuming but the power pulsing from it nearly took my breath away. As I stared, the stone shimmered and seemed to crack open soundlessly, turning into a dome of iridescent, near-blinding light. I turned my face away even as the witches sighed collectively, leaning towards it like people thirsting in the desert.

"Now," Whitaker's voice was soft but strong, "come forward, Witches, and partake of the Wellspring."

WHEN WE LEFT EARLY, no one objected, making Lydia promise to write notes on the meeting for us. Neither of us felt much up to anything more than sleep.

Well. Sleep after we talked.

"So, do you think my grandmother sent you the stranger's bell?" Whitaker asked.

"It makes more sense than it being my grandma. Yours was alive until just after the Autumnal Equinox. I got the snow globe close to the Equinox." I shrugged. "Makes sense."

"Lydia said Egon sang like a fish."

"What?"

"She mixes phrases up. Egon sang like a fish, she said. Under duress from the Unseelie, he told all. Or just about all. He wanted to make sure Demonborn were never welcome, so he framed the one Demonborn he had access to for the theft of the bells. That didn't work as well as he'd hoped, so he went on to plan B."

"Batshit crazy was plan B?"

"I didn't say it was a good plan."

"Why didn't he notice the thirteenth bell was missing before now?" I stretched out alongside him on the ridiculously posh hotel bed, wondering idly if I could slip the mattress into my luggage for the trip home.

"He had. He'd just hoped the fact you couldn't find it would make you look even guiltier." Whit barely stifled a yawn. "Damn it. I shouldn't be this tired right now."

"Are you fucking kidding me? Not only has this been possibly the most stressful week of our lives, it's the Solstice. The longest night of the year. The veil is thin and, hello? Witch? Even drawing from the Wellspring, you need your rest tonight. It's like...magical law or something."

He chuckled softly. "I wish we could be doing something else for the longest night and not sleeping." He gave his hips a lazy thrust against my ass, his mostly soft cock rubbing me in a promise of what we could do later, once we were both rested.

"There's always tomorrow," I murmured. "We have a lot of those."

CHAPTER TWELVE

The ghost of Solstice pluperfect

WHITAKER

At just past midnight, a knock fell on the hotel room door. Beside me, Rowan sprawled extravagantly across the bed, pushing me to the very edge with his starfish-splayed limbs. The knock fell again, and I knew I wasn't dreaming. Someone was actually bugging us at oh God thirty in the morning.

Slithering to my feet, I pulled on the jeans I'd discarded earlier, a bare nod to modesty given the hour and how few fucks I had left to give about anyone except Rowan. "Is someone dead?" I demanded as I opened the door.

The startled, wide-eyed gaze of the medium from earlier that evening stared back at me.

"Well, yes," he said, cracking a tiny smile. "Many people are dead. But two specifically would like to speak with you."

Rowan was half-awake and nursing a cup of hotel coffee as we settled around the room's tiny laminate-covered table. Despite the hour, Oscar Fellowes was cheerfully conscious, though I supposed that had something to do with his line of work and so many seances happening at night. "Common misconception," he said, and I realized I'd spoken aloud. "Most of mine occur during the late afternoon, but when we're filming, they happen at all hours. Not just the middle of the night." He sipped his coffee and made a face, which he quickly smoothed into polite lines. "Delicious," he lied.

"It's sludge," Rowan muttered. "No offense, Mr. Fellowes, I'm sure you're great at what you do and all, but if you're here trying to milk us for some sort of...whatever you call it, we're not interested." He slurped his coffee noisily before leaning over to rest his head on my shoulder.

"I'm here because your grandmothers would like to speak with you," he said gently. "And they are on a rather short schedule. They'd like to cross on."

Rowan sat bolt upright. "Cross on? She's...I mean...I thought..."

Fellows shook his head. "They've been waiting on you both," he said softly. "They love you very much."

The tip of Rowan's nose was red, and his eyes were bright with tears. "Can she hear me? If I talk to her, can she hear me, or do I have to go through you?"

Fellowes's gaze shifted to somewhere on Rowan's left. "She's right here. Go on."

Scooting back in his seat, Rowan turned to face the spot Fellowes had been staring at. "Grandma," he said softly, starting to reach out as if to touch her before tucking his hands under his legs. "Grandma...what the Hell?"

Fellowes's startled cackle broke the solemnity of the moment. "She's laughing, too. Says that she knew you and Whitaker would get on like a house on fire."

"Well," I said, "she's not wrong."

Rowan blushed. "Did you and Madame Frost seriously plan this all out?" he demanded. "How could you keep this so quiet?"

Fellowes listened for a long moment, then nodded. "Okay," he said quietly, then turned to Rowan. "She and Madame Frost knew it would take a miracle to get a Demonborn involved in the Council, even one as willing as you turned out to be, Rowan. They hoped a little nudge would help things along with the Witches."

"They couldn't have known I'd bleed on the stranger's bell," Rowan protested.

"Knowing my grandmother," I murmured, "she'd have found a way to ensure it."

Fellowes smirked and wagged one long finger at me. "You're next." Rowan sniffed, unable to stop a few tears from falling. He knew, I realized, that meant he only had a precious few moments left with his own grandmother, such as they were.

I excused myself into the en suite, running water so he could have some privacy. After a few minutes, he knocked on the door and edged in, red-faced and puffy-eyed. "You're up," he muttered, gently shrugging me off when I reached for him. "In a bit," he promised. "In a bit."

Fellowes was sitting just where I'd left him, murmuring to someone I couldn't see. He shook his head slightly and frowned before turning to face me. "Sorry, had a bit of a pop in. I had to tell them I'd speak with them later."

"Does that happen often?"

He quirked a brow at me. "I take it you don't watch much reality TV?"

It hit me, then, why he looked so familiar. "*Medium at Large*. You and that professor, the skeptic!"

He grinned. "That's Julian. We've been at it two years now, and I've only just started working for..." He trailed off. "Wow. That feels so odd to say. The Council. It's one thing being able to see and speak with souls, but knowing I'm the very bottom rung of a very tall ladder of...whatever we are... Yikes."

I didn't have the heart to tell him most supernaturals would never consider him to be one of us, rather just a slightly more evolved human. Instead, I smiled and rapped my knuckles on the table. "Welcome to the club, I guess?"

He snorted. "For the record, your grandmother informs me I'm not a member of the club but rather just a very special, albeit mundane human."

"Thanks, Grandmere," I sighed. "I was trying to be polite."

Fellowes snorted again. "She says being polite is for children and funerals; this is neither."

Tears I thought I was done shedding pricked my eyes. "Hi, Grandmere. I miss you."

"She says there's no need. Hm. Very...forthright, isn't she?"

"She was. Is?"

"Is," Fellowes said. "Definitely is. Death is..." He sighed. "Sorry, sorry. I'm to save my spiel for my own time, apparently, and not ramble on her watch."

I nodded. "Sounds right."

Fellowes leaned in, his expression kind. "She's on your right."

I nodded again and turned. "Hi," I said again. "You've really caused a lot of trouble, Grandmere..."

BY SOME UNSPOKEN AGREEMENT, Rowan and I did not talk about what our grandmothers shared in private. Part of me was bursting to know, to compare notes, but it felt too raw whenever I started to mention it. Fellowes had promised he'd see us again, and that our grandmothers were safe and happy and would cross over since they felt they'd done what they needed to do.

"You know," Rowan said as we drove back from dinner the night after Fellowes's visit, "I really don't think they'll cross. They're too invested in this shit."

It was the closest either of us had come to mentioning specifics. "Well," I said slowly, turning the car carefully into the hotel's parking lot, "we can always ask Fellowes later if he has any messages for us."

Rowan hummed thoughtfully. "I'm sure he'd tell us if he did."

On the walk back to the room, we were quiet. My thoughts bounced between my grandmother's visit, the upcoming Council meeting in a few days, and what I wanted to happen next with Rowan. Once back in the room, he sprawled on the bed again and turned his face towards me. "Can I just say...until I'm sure they're gone, I'm gonna be real weird about being naked."

"Oh, my gods," I groaned. "You don't think they..."

"I didn't until now! Ew!"

We shared the bed that night but kept a grandmother-safe six inches between us.

Epilogue

Jingle My Bells

ROWAN

"If you really loved me," Whitaker began. I silenced him with a well-placed throw pillow to the face.

Twice.

"I'm just saying," he laughed, dodging the third pillow, "if you really loved me, you'd wear the sweater."

"If you really loved me," I mimicked, "you wouldn't ask me to wear the sweater!"

"All I'm saying is that if we have to go to this meeting, we might as well have some fun with it." He produced the sweater, tossed at the foot of the bed a few hours before, and shook it at me. "C'mon, for me?"

"Come on it for you? Well, I mean, if you're into that sure, I'll give it a try, but I can't say it really revs my engine. Ow!" Pro-tip: Getting hit in the face with a jingle bell sweater hurts. "Clothes shouldn't jingle, Whitaker!"

He cackled, Witch that he was, and rolled out of bed. Bastard knew the best way to win an argument with me was to be naked. Pausing in the bathroom doorway, he shot me a look over his shoulder. "Think of it this way: you wear the sweater to the meeting, and later, I'll take it off you. Then you can take all your frustrations about jingling clothes out on me in bed."

I looked down at the blue-and-red sweater in my hands. "It's itchy, though," I muttered. We both knew full well I was going to put it on, despite the fact it was a disgusting sixty-three degrees outside and a t-shirt would suffice. "It'll make me feel all prickly." I looked back at him and sighed. "If anyone asks, you used some Witch charm bullshit on me."

Whitaker chuckled, disappearing into the bathroom and closing the door behind him even as I tugged the sweater over my head.

FROST HOUSE LOOKED as higgledy-piggledy yet imposing as the last time I'd seen it, though now it wasn't rimed in snow and hung with garlands and sparkling Witch-lights. Now, its slate roof was dark gray with damp, and the fluffy snow of the Solstice had given way to the hard, crunching ice of full-on winter. A tangle of mistletoe, holly, and ivy still hung over the door, the remnants of the kissing ball from a few weeks ago.

I hesitated, looking up at the greenery, still faintly sparkling with the collected magic of twelve Witch clans and one Demon. I tottered on the edge of the step before Whitaker's arm curled around my back, tugging me in close to his side. "Sorry," I muttered. "I'm still a bit gun-shy after the Solstice."

Whitaker batted the bedraggled ball, setting it swinging. Silvery sparks, remnants of the Solstice ritual magic, scattered over us like snowflakes. Everywhere they touched me, they spread a bloom of warmth, sending tendrils down to my bones. "You're invited this time," he pointed out. "And if anyone tries to give you shit about it, I'll turn 'em into a newt for you."

"Aw, but I like newts."

"Then I'll turn them all into newts and buy you a nice tank where you can lord it over them till the end of time."

"Aw, you do love me."

He turned abruptly, pulling me against his chest and kissing me hard and fast. "Never doubt that, Rowan. Ever. Now," he added with a swift smack on my backside, "let's get this over with. I want to get back home before New Year's."

Home. My home, now our home, since he'd decided to move to Houston instead of staying in the frozen north. He liked to say it was because he preferred heat to cold, but I had a fairly good feeling he just wanted us both away from his mother and Egon for the time being. At least until matters were settled with the Grand Council, and Demonborn knew where we stood for sure and for certain.

Everyone was assembled in the ballroom again, just like at the Summer and Winter Solstices. This time, though, there was no glossy oak tables or ornately carved ice sculptures. Just rows of folding chairs that looked uncomfortable as all Hell. "Let us begin," a petite, elegant Witch with very intimidating nails announced, stepping onto a plastic box so she could be seen by all assembled. "As was decided at the Winter Solstice meeting, we will welcome Rowan Hebert as a provisional member of the Grand Council."

A few polite claps and a muffled throat clearing sounded throughout the room. I sat stiffly, looking straight ahead at the Witch speaking.

"On the matter of the Revelation, it has been decided to delay the proceedings for a year and a day, then revisit the matter with the intent to vote. In the intervening time," she said, raising her voice to be heard over the low rush of conversation sweeping through the room, "we will be accepting four representatives from the Demonborn to act as liaisons between the Grand Council and the Watchers, as the Demonborn have been known to us in our history. Their duties will be further laid out in our next meeting after the new year."

She waited until the murmurs settled before pressing onward. "It has also been decided that Alastor Hebert will spearhead the investigation into the Humans First movement and their apparent knowledge of magical beings in the human world." She tapped one of those impressively long nails against her hip. "From what we have learned so far, the knowledge Humans First has of us speaks to a leak among the magical clans. Someone, or someones, are giving them information." Here, her gaze flicked towards me, and she flashed me a small, tight smile. "Alastor Hebert will not be brought on as a Council member, provisional or otherwise, but is offering his services voluntarily to ensure the safety of his brother and all Demons, after the events of this winter involving Mr. Paulson, Ms. Post, and their associates."

A shudder ran through me. The attempt on Whitaker's life had been terrible enough, but the knowledge the Council had been more than ready to blame me for it and see me tried and punished without hesitation made me uneasy. Without being told, I knew, no matter what the outcome of the Revelation, Demons would never truly be welcomed amongst the other supernaturals.

She digressed to discuss further business with regards to fundraising efforts and breakaway groups to work on projects for various sacred sites and safe houses, and then finally, they were done. Whitaker leaned over and whispered to me, "Do you want to stay for drinks and cake?"

"No," I sighed. "I really want you to take me back to the hotel and get this damned sweater off me."

He laughed, loud and long, standing to pull me into his arms and lifting me off my feet, so the bells hung on my sweater jingled. "Come on," he said, ignoring the looks being thrown our way. "I'll help you out of that if you help me out of these pants."

"It's a deal."

Books by Meredith:

You can find all my books listed on www.booksbymeredith.com[1] with links to buy at your favorite online retailers, or ask your local booksellers to order you a copy if you prefer!

The Bedeviled Series

The Devil May Care

The Devil You Know (December 2021)

The Devil in the Details (December 2021)

Speak of the Devil (Spring 2022)

Medium at Large Series

Bump in the Night

Ghoul Friend

Old Ghosts (December 2021)

In the Spirit (Spring/Summer 2022)

Book Five Title TBA (Fall/Winter 2022)

Science of Magic Series

Data Sets

Fuzzy Logic

Discrete (December/January 2021)

Book Four TBA (Spring 2022)

Stand Alones

Between the Lines (Contemporary MM Romance, March 2022)

Ring My Bell (Contemporary MM Fairy Tale Retelling, May 2022)

Leo (A Gaynor Beach Single Dads Romance, November 2022)

Dash (An apocalyptic romance with a HEA, October 2022)

Watch this space for more to come in 2022 and 2023...

---

1. http://www.booksbymeredith.com/

About the Author

Meredith likes to write about sexy stuff, weird stuff, and sometimes weird stuff doing sexy stuff. Originally from Texas, they live elsewhere now with their family and two cats who think they are gods (the cats, not the humans—the humans know their place).

Meredith writes queer-centered romances in various subgenres including paranormal, speculative fiction/alternate universe, contemporary, and historical. They firmly believe in happily ever afters and pineapple on pizza.

For sneak peeks at upcoming works and other goodies, check out Meredith's social media, Ko-Fi, and reader group.

Where to find me

Www.facebook.com/groups/meredithsreadingranch[1]

www.twitter.com/meredithspies[2]

www.facebook.com/meredithspiesauthor[3]

www.instagram.com/meredithspies[4]

https://bingebooks.com/author/meredith-spies

You can also find me on Ko-Fi, where I post serialized stories before they're available to the public, cover reveals, and more: www.ko-fi.com/booksbymeredith[5]

1. http://www.facebook.com/groups/meredithsreadingranch
2. http://www.twitter.com/meredithspies
3. http://www.facebook.com/meredithspiesauthor
4. http://www.instagram.com/meredithspies
5. http://www.ko-fi.com/booksbymeredith

www.ingramcontent.com/pod-product-compliance
Ingram Content Group UK Ltd.
Pitfield, Milton Keynes, MK11 3LW, UK
UKHW042019190726
13854UKWH00005B/2368

9 798201 696559